MINOR SNOBS

DANIEL AMORY

About the Author

Daniel Amory, an award-winning writer, was born in Chicago, Illinois in 1975. He made his first foray into writing as a Staff Writer for *The Daily Cardinal* while in college at the University of Wisconsin-Madison. In the fall of 1998, he began to work professionally as a journalist in connection with *The New York Times Magazine, A&E Television* and *The History Channel*, producing numerous documentaries seen worldwide.

Daniel lives in Chicago with his wife, Jennifer. They are regular contributors to many community and philanthropic activities.

Visit Daniel Amory's Websites At:

Facebook:
http://www.facebook.com/profile.php?id=100001730901052#!/pro file.php?id=100001730901052

Amazon:
http://www.amazon.com/DanielAmory/e/B004GFI3CW/ref=ntt_at hr_dp_pel_pop_1

Twitter:
@danielamory

Blogspot:
http://danielamory.blogspot.com/

To my wonderful parents
with admiration and love

I have had conflicting thoughts as to whether I should write about last summer because whenever you write about friends you feel a sort of breach in what is a series of spoken confidences. I understand that you may judge Connor, for instance, solely on how I depict him. As unjust or just as that is, this is unsought. In fact, many times I ruled out writing about him out of fear of such judgment by those who don't know him like I do.

A victim of my own curiousness, when I think back, I have wondered how I could have ever been so obviously brash in the face of infinite hope. But one man's intimate dream is another man's temporary preoccupation. There have been times I have thought some dreams should never be dreamt, but I would hate a world where that was true. I realize now that I do not accuse Connor or Griffin or any of the others of anything but something minor and I have come to this conclusion: We are all marred people—some are just preyed on more than others.

My family was borne generations ago from a continent out east in a city whose country depended upon the year. Birth certificates kept in vaults had shown Warsaw, Russia for each of my grandparents but for my maternal grandmother, who was born in Baltimore. My parents, both having been born in Chicago, unknowingly grew up two blocks away from each other and were living very separate lives until they met one night at a party.

My mother was an artist and a housewife and she excelled in both but only dreamt of one while the other always slowed those dreams. My father was a chemical engineer and worked for a big company developing food products and any entrepreneurial self that I have spirited over the years comes from him.

My sister, Barbara, was the first of us in the next generation to be born and everyone says she looks a lot like our Great Aunt Rebecca. Two years later, it was my brother, Adam, and he supposedly looks like my mother's brother, Uncle Richard. Finally, rounding out the three of us, I came in '82 looking like the re-birth of my father.

I graduated from Madison in 2003, and after toiling around as a journalist for three years in the dying profession of newspaper writing while still living in my parents' house in the outlying northern suburbs of this great metropolitan city by the lake, I went to law school where, I thought, I would have endless wisdom pitched at me in exacting throws.

Shortly before school started, I moved into a studio apartment on a quiet street near the bustle of the downtown in one of the most self-conscious bends of the world. The "Gold Coast" was a neighborhood that stretched five blocks along the lake in a sliver of land just south of Lincoln Park and north of River North. The streets were like fine necklaces and strung together were the brownstone houses and tall condominiums and tiny mansions like pearls, and when the day broke and the sun faded away, their lights burned like jewels shining gaudily in the night.

The world's most elegant bazaar, Michigan Avenue, jutted out from its eastern tip near The Drake Hotel and the timeless blue-green waters of Lake Michigan pressed its shores. The fractious make-up of the people that inhabited it, the flat squareness of its parks and the hint of the lake at the ends of its tree-lined streets squeezed together a domesticated cesspool of age and wealth and standing. It was a place one could readily dress up for an expensive dinner at one of the fashionable restaurants or have a drink miles high in the lounge of the looming John Hancock Building and five minutes later be out walking on the beach with pants cuffed and feet in the cool water at the lake's edge.

As I settled into my new surroundings, I started to feel like I was in the epicenter of a riotous new beginning and on the outside looking in at a vaudeville act at the same time and though I had the intention of placing in the top ten percent of my class like some of my peers, who ended up with high-salaried jobs at big firms waiting for them after graduation, I had a tough first semester and struggled slowly to climb to modest success.

On one pleasant spring night following graduation, I went to a rooftop party at my friend Griffin's building in Lincoln Park a block down from where Wrightwood met Clark Street. He was one of my closest friends throughout law school and with our last names next to each other in the alphabet, the prior week we had walked across the stage of the Arie Crown Theater at McCormick Place one after the other to take hold of that great parchment of paper that was the promised gold at the end of the law school rainbow.

There was loud music floating through the warm nighttime air as I rode in almost footless steps across the green cut lawns in a flare of red and orange sunlight splashing through trees to the gate at the foot of the front walk.

I climbed the stairs to the rooftop and opened the door to the deck. There were about twenty people at the party gathered in little groups; most of them were faces I knew from law school. On my right, I saw Griffin with a beer in his hand and sunglasses on standing in profile. As soon as he saw me he waved his beer toward me and then excused himself from a conversation and came around to greet me.

"Hey, Griffin," I said, extending my hand.

"Glad you could make it, Tom," said Griffin, shaking my hand.

He took his sunglasses off and clipped them to the collar of his shirt.

"How was L.A.?" I asked, observing his deep, dark tan.

He smiled widely and handed me a beer from a cooler.

"Tell me about the wedding," I said.

"Well, I made out with a bridesmaid," he said, laughing. "Um, we drank wine all weekend. I think my parents think I'm an alcoholic now."

"Why?" I asked.

"Because I kind of passed out at the wedding," he said.

"Passed out?" I said.

"Well, we were drinking wine all weekend," he said.

"Have you talked to the bridesmaid since?" I asked.

"No," he said. "I barely remember who she is. I barely know the bride."

"How was she related?" I asked.

"She was some friend of the bride," he said. "I don't think my cousin even knew her."

"Was the reception outside?" I asked.

"It was all outside," he said. "It was perfect. It's always sunny in California."

He paused long enough to sip his beer.

"You should have seen it," he started, "I got into a huge fight with my sister-in-law."

He smiled as if in varied thought.

"As you know, my family is very liberal and she's the only one who is a Republican and I hate her anyway," he said. "I mean why does she have to be so outspoken?"

He wiped sweat from his forehead.

"We were all drinking wine and we were a little loose," he said. "I think my sister hates her now which makes it worth it."

A tall girl with dark hair approached from behind and whispered something in Griffin's ear.

"I'll be back," he said a bit unevenly. "A little emergency in the kitchen."

As I stared at the red and orange clad sky, there was a promise of the summer ahead in the air and you could feel it. It was a promise with infinite possibilities if you could only believe in it. I walked slowly breathing in the warm air while looking out at the tilt of the trees in the distance. Groups of changing people in designer shirts and subtly drawn smiles passed around me in idleness and drunken laughter.

It was a generation growing in its disillusionment about the deepening recession and the backroom handshakes and greedy deals for private little pots of gold that created the largest financial meltdown since the Great Depression. As heirs to the throne, we all knew, of course, how bad the economy was, and our dreams, the ones we were told were all right to dream, were teetering gradually toward disintegration. However, on that night, everyone seemed physically at ease and exempt from life's worries with final exams over and bar class a distant dream with a week before the first lecture, and as I looked around at the jubilant faces and loud voices, if you listened carefully enough you could almost hear the culmination of three years in the breath of the night gasp in an exultant sigh as if to say, "Law school was over at last!"

"What have you been up to?" asked a man with sunglasses, who was shaking hands with a man wearing a blue collared shirt.

"Just hanging out," said the man in the blue collared shirt.

"Do you want to achieve something or do you just want to make money?" asked a nearby man in a white shirt to another man in a striped shirt. I waited for the answer as I slowly walked past them.

"Why is it an either or question?" the man in the striped shirt finally murmured philosophically under a sip of beer. They both stood there looking at each other in thought.

Gossiping sets splintered around me; up against the railing, I saw Jim Gibbs, who was in a suit and tie looking out at the spread of the city. Gibbs had graduated and passed the bar exam the previous summer and was now working at a medium-sized litigation firm in the city. He was married and had a one-year-old daughter. It was hard to realize that a man about my age had already brought another life into this world and was responsible for it.

"Glasses," I said extending my hand as I approached.

"Tom," said Gibbs, shaking my hand in a great smile.

"I like them," I said. "You look extra smart. I don't mean you look unintelligent every other day. You just look extra smart."

"We have a big trial," he started. "I wear glasses when we're in trial. I want to look extra smart. Every advantage helps."

He turned away and looked out at the blurred lights in the wake of the descent of the twilight while I joined him at the railing.

"When do you start at the City?" he asked.

"Monday," I said.

"And it's paid?" he asked.

"It's part-time while I study for the bar," I said.

He nodded absently.

"Oh, by the way, I got that questionnaire from the state bar asking me to be a reference," he said. "I sent it in last week."

"Thanks," I said.

He nodded absently again.

"I'm glad you could take off a little early and make it tonight," I said.

"Yeah, well, nobody was there today," he said, taking his glasses off and wiping them lightly against the cuff of his sleeve.

"Really, nobody was there?" I asked.

"Well, nobody important," he said, putting his glasses back on and blinking.

There was a pause as he settled back into a stare of the beyond.

"You know, sometimes I think this is just not it," he said, his glasses flashing from the early night's light.

He turned toward me in a thoughtful pause.

"You know what I mean, Tom?" he asked. "It's just not."

"What happened?" I asked.

"Nothing happened," he said.

He wiped away sweat pooling above his brow.

"Actually, today is just flying by," he said. "Colleen gave me some medical records to review and medical records just eat up hours. They're the best."

He sighed.

"I think I'll make my billables for the week," he said. "It's just one day you're up and the next you're—it's tough. It's the hardest thing to do. Litigation is the hardest thing."

He wiped his brow again.

"I'm a competitive person, but—the work is fine—it's the office politics," he said, finally. "The cliques."

He looked out at the city and then back toward me.

"If I knew in law school what I know now," he said. "I'm starting to look. Becker getting that corporate thing inspired me to look. But there's not much out there and with Kara, I can't really take a chance."

As the night went on, the fickle twilight slowly faded into a night of blackness with fireflies lighting the warm air with balls of light. The stars glittered in the sky and as the number of people at the party grew there were merging conversations and laughter and bodies moving in outlines around the kegs of beer in a curtsy of youth.

I drifted dreamily along and as the blackness of the night receded higher and higher into the sky, the lights of the city blazed in blurred light along the streets below, broadening the expanse of the city, and giving depth to what would ordinarily be a scene without contrast.

"I was a pre-school teacher for a year before law school, and so I thought I wanted to do family law, but I clerked at the Public Guardian's office last summer and I realized I didn't want to do that," said Gwynn, whose slender frame leaned slightly over the railing of the balcony. We had just met at the party the previous moment.

"These kids, many of them didn't trust anyone and they had already been to a few other foster homes," she said, looking up at me steadily.

I nodded with great interest.

"If things were going well, you'd see if the parents were at the point of wanting to adopt the child," she said. "If things weren't going well, which was more often the case, you'd have to try and see what you could do that was best for the kid."

She paused and as a breeze swept over the rooftop, she pushed back her long blonde hair. In the moonlight, her earrings dangled faint circular shadows on her bronzed skin.

"These homes were usually not in the safest neighborhoods and the attorneys would have to drive out there themselves," she said. "You were trained in how to interview the children. You'd ask about their DCFS agent and usually the DCFS agents did nothing. I mean, it's so slow to get anything done. A kid needs a bus pass. You'd think you could just get the bus pass from the DCFS. Nope. Everything takes so much time. These cases go on for years."

She pushed back her hair.

"Do you live with a roommate?" she asked suddenly.

"No," I said, turning my head side to side. "You?"

She nodded.

"And a dog."

She smiled.

"My crazy dog," she said. "Mitchell."

"What kind of dog is Mitchell?" I asked.

"He's a Pomeranian mix," she said. "He has a stupid haircut. I have a picture."

She pressed a couple of buttons on her cell phone. As a picture of her dog flashed on the screen, she turned it toward me. "It's the lion look," she said. "You can have a lion or a teddy bear look and I hate the teddy bear look and it's hard to manage." I stared keenly at the picture.

"He looks possessed there, but usually he's pretty cute," she said.

"Did you have a dog growing up?" I asked.

"No," she said. "My dad said he was allergic and recently we found out that was all a lie."

She laughed.

"My dad, he doesn't like to get dirty," she said.

She turned the phone back toward her.

"Here's another picture," she said, after pressing several more buttons.

"I know I have all of these pictures up on Facebook, but I guarantee you I'm actually an old soul," she said.

As she turned the phone toward me, I examined the picture.

"Sometimes I think people are just going to stop hanging out one day," she said. "We're just going to sit in a room in front of Facebook and interact on-line."

She laughed.

"I say this yet I admit I'm addicted to it," she said. "I never should have signed up."

A moment later another picture of her dog flashed on the screen. As she turned the phone toward me, I studied it closely.

"It's funny because he does not recognize that he's a dog here," she said. "Because he's really cute and looks like a little lion, when people see him they're like, 'Oh, he's really cute.'"

Her eyes rested on the picture for a moment.

"Obviously," she said, "he doesn't understand what they're saying and I know he doesn't understand what I say to him, but I'm so used to him being in the house that I talk to him and when I have friends come over they're like, 'You know you're having a conversation with your dog?'"

In the moonlight, there was a shadow of a man with his head bent down typing a message into his cell phone beneath the magical shine of the glittering stars lighting the sky to whoever that lay awake in the night at the other end. At the time, I didn't know who it was—it was just an outlined shadow and like all shadows it was mysterious and the person behind it unknown. I looked out at the expanse of lights drawn riotously across the city's streets. Feeling the breeze slightly up off the lake, I glanced back toward the shadow, but it was gone.

That weekend the city blushed with a great heat wave but on Monday it rained, cooling the ache in the street's burn. It was the first day of my clerkship at the City and rifts of gray broke the sky with a darkening glum, hiding the tops of buildings behind thick storm clouds. The rain hit off the fronts of buildings, and as it dripped from the hems of awnings, the wet sidewalks glistened with blurred reflections. Headlights of cars in endless traffic shined brightly in streaks of yellow light as puddles pooling along the sides of intersections provided an early morning obstacle course. The fogged windows of passing buses hinted of crowded aisles as arms dressed in raincoats held umbrellas over faces with only eyes.

As the light on the corner changed, I hurried across the street with the procession of umbrellas and huddled overcoats and hoods. Looking straight ahead, my thoughts crept in a fragmented manner to law school, and as a vague stillness arose, I was professedly forgetting all of my achievements and fixating on only the failures. In my infantile wisdom, I soared eagerly above a puddle of unknown depths at the foot of the curb only to step right in the middle of it, splashing at the feet of a mass of rushing shoes. Pressing on in the crowded march with wet pant cuffs, I noticed my hand was red from gripping the umbrella too tightly. As I looked down at full skylines in the bright reflections of deep puddles, I could hear the draining of the water in the street. Under the sound of a train going by in front of the office building, I pushed the glass of the revolving door forward in a spirited jilt and emerged in a hiccup as the rush of cold air from the lobby collided with the warm pilfering air seeping inside. After shaking my umbrella on the giant brown carpet lining the pathway by the doors, I checked in at the front desk. With a name tag attached to the breast of my coat, I walked with wet feet to the elevator and pressed the UP button and waited for one of the eight elevators in the long drawn hallway to open its doors and whisk me up to the office in a sudden expulsion.

At eight-thirty, Jerry Moss, a senior attorney in the division, met me by the reception desk. He was in his early fifties and had a pinkish, child-like face, average height and build, and receding red hair. As he stood upright in a somewhat timid stance with his hands balled in his suit coat pockets, it occurred to me that I had seen him before—free-lancing around the varied backdrops of the Gold Coast alone—but this was all before that day when I actually met him.

We shook hands and as I waited for him to say something, I realized that he had never really seen me before. It was at that point he turned me around and led me through the office in a parade like I was King Richard and I was being shown the village from the Sherwood Forest for the first time. As it was still early, a glut of noiseless echoes borrowed from a night of nothingness bathed the empty hallway as distant sounds gained importance. The thin gray tapestry in the halls and offices was sporadically dotted with shapeless dark blemishes hinting of many long winters. There were computer screens flashing radiant light on its pale faced users, clicking on keyboards and creaking of bodies shifting ever so lightly in padded desk chairs. There were big firm oak desktops with papers scattered and in piles, folders with case names neatly packed in large steel filing cabinets, hooks with dripping overcoats on backs of doors and the dull grayness from the small etched windows that led to the world outside.

Jerry sat down behind his wide oak desk in his large, corner office and as I sat down in the chair opposite him he told me that he was recently new to the division, himself, after having transferred from Employment Litigation. I asked why he transferred divisions.

"I wanted a warm and inviting place," he said, folding his little hands neatly together. "I was ready for a change."

I looked at the array of magnets on the side of his desk which were, presumably, placed there to serve as conversation starters; one was from Argentina, one from St. Louis, and one from Cancun. I then glanced at the Chicago Cubs coffee mug sitting on his desk.

"I take it you're a Cubs fan," I said.

"That's a bingo," he said. "Are you?"

"Oh, yeah," I said, nodding. "It seems like they can't win lately though."

"Yeah, when they're playing like this, they lose the games like yesterday," he said. "When they are playing well, they win them."

"How many games do you go to a year?" I asked.

"Thirteen," he said. "It's the funniest thing. My partner—she married the beer vendor in our section."

"Really?" I said.

"Yeah," he said. "She likes beer and she liked the beer vendor and it's a fairy tale story, really."

He paused for breath.

"You know," he said in an attempt to whet my taste, "one of those tickets may have your name on it this summer. We'll have to see how it all shakes out."

I instantly got the feeling that he said that to everyone in order to try and gain acceptance. Later, I heard that Jerry had had lunch at the Allegro Hotel that week with Steven, an attorney in the division, and that at one point Jerry had told him, "I heard you are an Indians fan...I have season tickets with the Cubs...the Indians are coming to Wrigley this year." Steven said he quickly changed the subject and asked Jerry about the kind of cases he tried when he was in Employment Litigation.

"I didn't want to lead him on like we were going to be hanging out or anything outside work," Steven had privately told me.

Steven said Jerry had wanted to be the "go to guy" right away following his transfer and that it was hard for him to take a backseat at first, but then he realized it was for the better.

In time, I would soon get the impression that Jerry's sole sense of self worth was attached to his position at the City and that it was his only escape from his extreme loneliness. I think he knew this and clung to his title and the amassed respect that came along with it like it was his lifeline to the real world he was not part of, but desperately wanted to be.

"Oh, are you going to go to that happy hour tonight?" he asked me one day in a sociable way.

"I think I'm going to go for a little while," I said. "What about yourself?"

"I'd like to, but I can't," he said. "I have a spinning class and it's actually for the benefit of the entire division. You see, if I go to the spinning class tonight, I win a large sweets basket from State Street Bakery."

He hesitated for a moment as if he was waiting for my reaction.

"They have a promotion going on at my gym this week," he began again. "If you go to a spinning class three times you get a small sweets basket from State Street Bakery and if you go to five classes, you get a large basket. Tonight will be my fifth class.

Actually, it's my fourth class, but my instructor punched my card twice yesterday."

"On purpose or accidentally?" I asked.

"On purpose," he said with boyish eagerness. "She likes me. I go to her class every week. Never five times in one week before though, or, rather, four times."

He paused a moment.

"She actually has the class go for an hour and fifteen minutes," he said. "Nobody has to do a spinning class for an hour and fifteen minutes, but I believe if you're in the class you follow the instructor. I think that's why she double punched my card. It's actually five classes in four."

"What's the retail price on a sweets basket like that?" I asked.

"I'm not sure," he said. "But it's State Street Bakery."

He attempted a fumbling gesture.

"It serves twenty people," he said. "There are brownies and cookies. There are probably others things too."

He cleared his throat.

"The whole division will benefit," he said. "I'll probably bring it in next Friday. I think I'll have to order it first. I'd like to call a meeting and have everyone come into the conference room and take something."

He looked at me intently.

"Make sure you take something when I bring it in," he said.

I think I will take a moment and tell you about how my days were usually spent during this time. By nine o'clock in the morning, everyone was tucked away in their office, checking and responding to their e-mail. Most days I would sit stationary at my desk for long stretches of time writing motions for cases in varying stages of litigation. In many instances, the supporting documents had been scanned and were available on-line and were downloaded and included as evidence. Sometimes, however, if the case had a difficult issue attached to it, I would have to run over to the

Recorder of Deeds in the basement below City Hall and hold my breath from the lasting foul stench that dated back to the "flood" years ago and pull certain documents because they wouldn't be available otherwise.

After the noon rush had been stuffed and the crescendo of the lunch hour died down, I would usually get a turkey and mayonnaise sandwich with other law clerks from the deli around the corner and have conversations about politics and sports and law school. Sometimes, on Tuesdays, I would go to the fast food Mexican restaurant up the block for "Dollar Tacos," and sit along the square at Daley Plaza and watch the water fountain spout into the air with a background of the Chicago Picasso under long breaths as if in a trance while the sun warmed my face. In the afternoon, there was always one clerk who was coming or going to the frozen yogurt shop across the street. I began to go once a week and I would get the small vanilla cup with fresh strawberries and blueberries on top and eat it in a slow walk back to the office before the warm air could melt it.

In late May bar class started with fanfare and dread alike. Each day we were herded like cattle through lecture after lecture covering topic after topic in regularly rehearsed intervals. Eight subjects were covered in the multi-state multiple choice portion of the exam, the remaining covered in the essay part. If you went to the morning class, you had the option of going to the live taping of the lecture in the main auditorium or watching a televised feed of the lecture in one of the classrooms. If you went to the afternoon class, you only had the choice of watching the re-play of the morning lecture in one of the open classrooms. I alternated between the two and would work at the City either in the morning or afternoon depending upon the lecture I would attend.

In the readiness of the coming evening, I would usually eat dinner frugally at one of the designated local hole-in-the-walls around my apartment and then sit in the hipster coffee shop on the corner of the street opposite a stretch of neon lights at my usual table against the window pawning hours studying my notes for an unknown future as the world around me seemingly rushed to enjoy the warm weather before fall could come along and spoil it. It was better to be inside the coffee shop enduring the cold rush of air from the air conditioner drinking hot coffee while studying than outside in the heat licking cold ice cream and walking through the streets. I would tell myself this almost every hour not to convince myself, but, well, actually it was to convince myself.

Sometimes I would take a break between hours and wander restlessly from street to street in a long walk young men with natural curiosities and scripted thoughts take when the dreams they have lent themselves to extend back to them in fast times. I would look inside store windows and pass random homeless people on the street begging for money as the twilight slowly faded into the burnt light of streetlamps in the night and then walk up Rush Street and watch the intricate gestures of the idling silhouettes of the dinner crowd sitting down at restaurants eating long decadent feasts absorbed with their idleness while imagining what they thought as they saw me.

I secretly envied and resented them, the men dressed in expensive suits without ties and the women with their fashionable dresses and sparkling jewelry, for their tacit aristocracy. Voices blended with faint background chatter as they formed prominent poses outlined by the moonlight; a TV journalist, a baseball star, and various social celebrities eating at elegant white clothed tables with warm bread and bottled water and silk napkins.

There were conversations that needed hands holding glasses of red wine to help make spirited points and superficial glances and pampered smiles from mouths discreetly finishing medium filets cooked in butter. I liked to circle the Triangle and casually loiter at a tiny outdoor coffee shop in its middle and try different flavored coffees in a surge of thought and worry, open and bound in contrast alike, while drifting through swelling groups and intimate conversations and looking up at the beautiful light of the stars in the sky.

There was a diner on the corner of North and Clark that was open all night long and many times I would sit inside there and order a dessert when I would study late at night. There was always an interesting late night crowd there eating greasy food and drinking bitter coffee, but they had big tables and good lighting and an outlet behind the booth in the back near the kitchen for my laptop and I would practice writing essays from topics I would blindly choose from my notes until that poignant moment when my eyes would start to close on their own.

May rolled swiftly by and on a Saturday in early June, Gwynn and I took a break from studying to walk through the Old Town Art Festival. The booths stretched four blocks from North Avenue to Division Street, each one with artwork, jewelry, crafts, wooden game boards, purses and pottery. Along either side of the street restaurants had opened their windows for lunch, lining the sidewalks with tables and flower beds. There were people sitting leisurely and eating ends of sandwiches held with tips of fingers and chatting and squinting from the sun.

Wedging his way past us in the other direction was a boy, who was around three years old, standing behind his own empty stroller, pushing it while his mother walked beside him. There were groups of women in summer blouses with string ties in the back and skirts with platform heels and tiny wrist wallets and knots of men in beer gardens posing with sunglasses and form-fitting T-shirts untucked and blowing gently in the wind, showing off well-built physiques from hours in the gym during the winter.

"Where have you been studying?" I asked Gwynn, a startling solitary vision among many moving backgrounds in the light of the afternoon.

"I have this spot in my office," she said, adjusting her sunglasses. "I have a place with my couch and my desk, a place for my water and all my books and papers. If anyone else were to walk inside, they'd think it was a mess, but to me it's perfectly organized."

We wandered slowly from booth to booth along the street.

"I put my books out for the day over here and my practice essays over there," she said, momentarily gesturing. "It makes sense to me."

She slipped her sunglasses off and set them at rest on the top of her head and then smoothed her hair with a hand.

"And I don't get distracted when I study in there," she said in a gratified way. "But I have to study in there."

As she walked forward her shoulders glistened in the sunlight. She looked at the street and then turned toward me.

"Anywhere else in my apartment and then you have the phone and the TV and my dog and my roommate."

She preceded me to one of the booths and leaned forward to examine a broach as it fell into her palm. Her earrings dangled down from her ears as she moved.

"My roommate, Andrea, still comes up to me every day and is like, 'I'm about to put a movie in if you want to—oh, I forgot, you're studying,'" she said, her eyes fastened on the broach as it sparkled a million sparkles in the light. "'You forgot?' I'd ask her. 'I've been studying for three weeks.' I tell her, 'You can have a movie on in the background because it won't distract me, but I just can't watch it with you.'"

I stood there following her movements with my eyes. As I studied the outlines of her body raised against the blaze of the sun's glare, she suddenly looked back toward me and caught me staring.

"I do get caught up with people watching at times I have to admit," she said, after a slight hesitation. "My office has a window that faces the street and I'll look out at the people passing."

She placed the broach neatly back onto its perch on the counter and turned toward me.

"On Tuesday, my neighbor across the street was outside and I suddenly looked over and there was an entire dining room table set on the front lawn," she said, again adjusting her sunglasses. "I was like, 'How did that get there?' A few minutes later, a van pulled up and hauled it away. I think she must have sold it to someone and they were coming to pick it up."

She paused for breath.

"It's funny, everyone who took the exam last year tells me that eventually you will hit a wall," she said without enthusiasm. "There will be one day when you hit a wall and lose it."

I listened intently.

"I was a representative for Kaplan in law school," she started, "and my co-worker was like, 'Oh, you're going to cry. There will be a day when you will cry.' I was like, 'I'm not a crier. I haven't cried before and I don't see myself crying about this.'"

She suddenly turned toward me.

"Where do you study?"

"Lately, I've been going to this hipster coffee shop near my apartment called Black Duck Coffee," I said, shifting from one foot to the other. "Have you heard of it?"

"No," she said with a tiny turn of her head.

"Yeah, nobody's heard of it," I said.

"Is anybody else studying for the bar there?" she asked, her hands resting on her hips.

"No," I said, leaning toward her. "It's funny. These girls who are the baristas that work there—they always give me these looks. They have this deal for $1.70. It's bottomless coffee. So I come in there with all my books and they give you this mug that you just re-fill and I sit there for like seven hours."

The nights in June were hot and the days hotter. In class, the students would increasingly sit in static, tiny hushed rows taking sprawling notes as distinguished professors with dully open mouths and less than thrilling voices spoke in exhaustive detail. Most of the students had attended mid-western law schools with only a handful of east coast schools and several from out west. I noticed that there was a mix of neurotic note takers with pressing lips and fright for eyes and on the other end, the relaxed sort, and somewhere among them I fit in.

One day, I went to the morning lecture and afterward I saw Griffin stiffly stand up and begin to gather his books in a row along the side of the stage in the auditorium. His friend standing by his shoulder was a stranger to me.

"Tom this is Connor, Connor this is Tom," said Griffin.

Connor was about five-seven with a stocky build. He casually offered his hand and I shook it.

"Listen, we're going to go study," said Griffin, as he gruffly slung his bag over his shoulder. "Why don't you come?"

"Where are you guys going?" I asked.

"This small coffee shop on State and Chestnut," said Griffin.

"All right," I said.

"Where have you been studying?" asked Connor.

"I go to this hipster coffee shop near my apartment called Black Duck Coffee," I said.

They both waved their heads side to side in synchronized turns as if neither had heard of it or, for that matter, even the word coffee before.

"Yeah, nobody's heard of it," I said.

Suddenly, Connor's phone vibrated. He quickly reached for it inside his pocket in a swift, drooling urgency that Pavlov, himself, could have only hoped for from his dogs. After reading the message with rapidly moving eyes, he politely excused himself and walked forward into the hallway. As I stood there and watched his shadowed outline in the distance, it occurred to me at that moment that Connor was the silhouette from the rooftop sending and receiving messages on his phone late into the night at Griffin's party earlier that spring.

Once on the bus, Connor started to tell Griffin about a woman who tried to join the KKK and then attempted to back out and was shot in the head.

"Isn't that sad?" asked Connor.

"I feel bad about it," started Griffin, "but I can't think about that otherwise I'll be depressed all the time."

Griffin looked out at the passing landscape through the large-framed window on his side of the bus.

"That gym," said Griffin, pointing to a small gym on the corner suddenly as if to occupy that space in his brain held temporarily by the story regarding the woman with a different thought, "the owner is from New York."

Griffin turned toward me.

"He was a lawyer. He took all of his money and opened one out there. This is the second one."

I stared at the gym through the window in passing.

"If I wasn't going to be a lawyer," said Griffin, "I think I'd go into business."

"What kind of a business?" I asked.

"A bagel shop," he said. "I'd call it Griffin's Bagels."

"What about Haley's Bagels?" I asked, referring to the name of his cat.

"Haley's Bagels is good," he said.

We decided to stop and get some lunch at a small café before studying. Set back from the street, there was a large outside seating area along the sidewalk carved out by red and yellow flowerbeds and a long outstretched awning. We proceeded past the outlying flowerbeds to a table that opened toward the corner of the street. As I sat down at the table, the breeze blew gentle sweeps of caught air past the awning while the sun shined down through the trees in a bright, slanted flare, tinting everything a slightly broad yellow hue.

"Don't you think most of those kids think too much about who got an A or a B when they were in law school and what that means to an inflated G.P.A. and not enough about the world?" asked Connor irrelevantly.

Just like with the question on the bus, Griffin gave no hint as to his desire to answer it. He gave a slight shrug of his shoulders and then looked lazily up at a completely motionless sky, straining his eyes from the sun's flare.

"Summer in Chicago," murmured Griffin in a romantic tone. "You know, I was studying out on my deck on Saturday and I got red and I've been getting it for my tan—people keep saying, 'How much are you actually studying?'"

Connor turned to Griffin.

"Tell him my rule about the beach and see what he thinks," he urged excitedly.

"You do it," demanded Griffin in a rather short tone.

Connor leaned forward as if he had something particularly important to tell me.

"Don't you think that the only people who should take their shirts off at the beach are people that are married, because they don't care, or people that are well-built?" he asked.

It seemed like a bizarre question to pose to someone he scarcely knew. I looked at Connor with a thoughtful pause.

"Connor is going to Madrid and I told him that he is going to be the only guy on the beach there with his shirt on," explained Griffin, attempting to provide some context.

"I'm not going to take it off," said Connor contemptuously.

"What are you so worried about?" I asked in a detached sort of curiousness.

"I'm going with a friend of mine," said Connor in earnest. "A good friend. A girl. And she's cute and fit."

Connor stared sharply at me.

"She is fit."

"It's a topless beach," said Griffin. "She's probably not even going to be wearing a shirt."

"So you're worried about—" I started to say.

"This," broke in Connor, patting his fleshy waist in a self-loathing manner.

"Maybe she's into that," I retorted.

"Get out of here," exploded Connor in fractious laughter as if she would forever be incapable of such a thing.

"At least wear a white T-shirt," said Griffin, flashing an unaffected grin. "A plain one."

Connor laughed again in the same fractious tone.

"I'm worried about it," groped Connor, his eyes more accentuated now. "I'm being serious. The beach worries me. I've gained some weight since she last saw me."

Before I could respond, he excitedly confessed, "I wouldn't care if I wasn't going with her."

"When do you go?" I asked.

"After the bar exam," said Connor.

"So, you have almost eight weeks?" I said.

At that very moment, an expression of infinite hope gripped his face, and though I didn't quite grasp the gravity of the moment at the time, I realize now that I had been a witness to the birth of the obsession that would turn his trip into one last desperate attempt to try and re-make the past and win back the girl of his dreams. I don't think Connor even knew it because it wasn't a new dream. It was more the realization of an unrealized dream from an old womb filled with regret, and as long as he had his phone, he was never too far from it—as real or unreal as it was.

"Should I have a doughnut or my disgusting cardboard?" asked Gwynn, as she drew up languidly before me at a study table in a bookstore on State Street, raising a puffed rice cake in the air.

My eyes narrowed attentively at her face, but as I hesitated, she announced eagerly, "Disgusting cardboard it is!"

She eased down into the chair opposite me, setting her flashcards in a tall pile on the table.

"It's not disgusting if you can eat it I guess," she informed me.

She leaned forward and took several books out from her backpack. Her proximity caused me to watch her twisting her body.

"I walked to class and back this morning," she said, whipping her hair around as she straightened her shoulders. "I think I got a tan on one arm."

She lifted her right arm and carefully inspected the rosy-colored tint to it.

"I just missed the showers," she said in afterthought.

She started to thumb through her flashcards while listening to the soft lingering music in the background.

As the day progressed, at one point she got up to get another coffee.

"What?" she asked as we exchanged a short glance.

"How many cups of coffee have you had?" I asked curiously.

"How do you think I get through so many flashcards so fast?" she asked, gesturing. "I have fifteen pounds of caffeine in my body."

Late in the afternoon, I got to my feet in a yawn and wandered off to the bathroom and when I returned to the table Gwynn was sending a text message on her phone to her friend, Jaclyn.

"Are most of your friends in the city law school friends?" I asked casually.

"All of them except for my roommate, Andrea," she said. "None of my friends from high school live in the city."

She paused a moment.

"We're all still tight, but most of them are either still back home or in New York," she remarked. "There's one girl from my high school who lives here, but she's married and has a kid and it's a totally different story."

She sipped her coffee with the tiniest of sips.

"My college friends—we talk about college all the time when we see each other," she continued. "We reminisce about the old days when we were young and stupid. It's just with my law school friends that we don't talk about law school."

She smiled faintly.

"I think we're all traumatized."

She leaned back in her chair.

"I would love to have my best friend live in the same city," she said suddenly. "I've known my best friend Melissa since grade school and I think if we were to live in the same city it would be so cool, but I think we would be like, 'Grow up already' after seeing each other act certain ways."

As the afternoon wore on and the sun started to sink down the horizon in little sprits of color, the streets started to get crowded. I watched people passing for awhile through the great window to the world before me and then looked back down drearily at my notes with visible effort. As dusk fell and the lights started to appear brightly from the glowing street lamps and early shining stars, Gwynn leaned forward and started to gather her books. She told me she was going to go home and have dinner and study the rest of the night in her office.

"Actually, I may stop off at Whole Foods," she said in a thoughtful pause. "Mitchell needs more of his organic chow mix. And I'm trying this high fiber diet. I'm eating this special cereal that is high in fiber, but not as sweet as Special K and I'm almost out."

She hesitated and as she did a single wrinkle appeared in the middle of her forehead.

"I've officially turned into a loser," she whispered cynically. "I'm looking forward to going home and having cereal for dinner and walking Mitchell and studying a little and then going to sleep. I've had my 'going out and having fun' quota for the year, I guess, and it's June."

She lifted her bag over her shoulder and turned around to face me.

"It's expensive to eat out anyway," she exclaimed.

She then picked up her coffee cup, raised her hand to wave and left.

A moment or two later, she trotted back into the bookstore.

"I don't know what I did with my umbrella," she said, embarrassed.

She leaned down and glanced around the table.

"It didn't just get up and walk away," she said, setting her coffee cup down on the table. "I'm sure it'll turn up."

I leaned forward and looked under the table with her.

"Oh, here it is," she said, bending along the window. "And it's right where I left it. Imagine that."

Turning around, she waved again and left.

Not one moment later she came silently prancing back inside the bookstore in an almost tiptoe. I sat there with fascinated eyes as she took a step forward to pick up the coffee cup she had left on the table.

"All right," she said, turning around. "I'm leaving for real now."

"When I was at Employment Litigation, I was in federal court, mostly," said Jerry one morning as we briskly walked through the metal detector at the Administrative Hearings building on Superior Street. "You never know how it's going to go there. They have little sympathy for the plaintiffs. There were several cases I thought I should have won, but didn't."

He smoothed his red tie a fraction with impersonal necessity. After a certain degree of smoothness, he stopped.

"I spent some time in state court too," he said. "I know a lot of judges."

As I followed Jerry through a crowded hallway of gathering police officers, there was an upsurge of joining noises.

"Administrative Hearings," he said in a scholarly voice, "is different than what I'm used to. As you will see, it's very casual and sometimes the Administrative Officers follow the law and sometimes they don't. Many times, they'll give second and third chances to people, which is a bit frustrating if you're the City trying to enforce the code, which we are."

We rounded the corner and as a dense mass of important-looking people in suits absorbed in their tiny surroundings passed, we started up another hallway.

"Sometimes, and I think we have several today, we pick up cases for other departments when we're here," he said, looking at me closely. "Just last week I was prosecuting a motion to set aside a default judgment against this father and son team who were attempting to scalp White Sox tickets and it was the son who was caught."

He rested his eyes on me as if they were flowing in thought.

"You can't scalp tickets a certain radius around the ballpark," he said with a small lift in his forehead. "And so I talked to the two of them during settlement negotiations before the trial and they kept changing their story two and three times and they were saying that they knew the cop and that he had had it in for them and so on and they asked for a deal and I put an offer on the table, but I told them if they didn't agree to it and instead decided to go to trial, I would pull it off the table."

He hesitated for a moment.

"So they decided to go in front of the judge and they changed their story a fourth time and the judge explained to them that we were not arguing the merits of the case, only why they didn't appear at the first hearing when they received a default judgment," he said.

He paused for a long breath a few feet from the courtroom.

"Anyway, they lost and afterward I was kidding with Steven back in my office, I said, 'I was going to argue that they should have been found guilty purely on the fact that they were trying to scalp White Sox tickets,'" he said under strange little grunts of laughter.

He stood there continuing to laugh to himself as he blew his nose into a handkerchief.

"White Sox tickets," he said again with several more excited grunts. "Do you get it? Because, you know, they've been having trouble selling tickets. Anyway, I remember, I joked later with the judge, I said, 'What do you call scalping White Sox tickets?' And he said, 'What?' And I said, 'Paying face value.'"

His smile came slowly as he studied my reaction. I quickly smiled to indicate that I was listening.

"The judge was a big Cubs fan," he added.

The next morning in class the professor, a man about sixty years old with a trimmed white beard and dark hallowed eyes, lectured benignly for three hours about estates and trusts in the stale air of the cheerless auditorium.

After class, I went with Griffin and Connor to the coffee shop on State and Chestnut to study for the afternoon under sporadic bouts of quietness and measured air. During a short break of drifting thought, Griffin, who had slightly dark circles under his eyes, turned toward me.

"Do you remember that bridesmaid I told you about from that wedding I went to in L.A.?" he asked.

"Yeah," I said, lightly nodding.

"It turns out that she actually lives in Chicago and she had the bride call my mother to get my phone number," he said, raising his eyebrows.

"She called your mother?" I asked in a somewhat surprised tone.

"Well, she had the bride call my mother," he said.

"What does she do?" I asked.

"She's in school to be a psychologist," he said. "We're going to hang out Friday night."

As the afternoon waned silently into night, Connor and I sat in varied poses of stillness after Griffin had gone home. Inside, the crowd was faintly drawn and it was quiet while outside under the streetlamps shadows dotting the sidewalks creased into darkness. As I sat there in shades of emotion, the night pressed on in surges of hopefulness following a well-written practice essay and near despair after several wrong multiple choice questions in a row.

At one point, I looked over at Connor and he was leaning forward still as still with marbled glazed eyes responding with the utmost precision to a message on his phone—one I knew had to have been sent by the girl driving his obsession. As I watched him disappear in thought, his facial muscles tightened into feverish expressions of ecstasy hinting a vivid reflection of his infatuation. Later, as the night faded out, I casually asked him about her.

"Her name is Courtney," he said, his pupils widening. "She was my closest friend in college."

He told me they first met on campus at the University of Michigan. Her dorm room was the one next to his on the third floor.

"We were best friends almost immediately," he said, reflective and depressed all within the same breath.

He said during their junior year they started dating.

"She's really smart," he said with a distant smile. "She's like one of the smartest people I know. She reads a lot, not only for school, but outside."

One night, he eagerly showed me an array of pictures of her on his phone from her Facebook profile.

"Isn't she cute?" he broke out excitedly.

There was a pause of great consequences as I studied her delicate features. After a few more seconds of silence, I realized that he actually wanted me to say something.

"Yeah," I said, finally.

He stared at me for a long moment as if I should have been more exuberant.

"This picture is better," he said suddenly. "The ones of her outside kind of washes her out. This one shows her coloring better. I actually posted it. Isn't she cute?"

The picture displayed a closer view of her delicate features.

"She's cute," I said.

"She's cuter than this other girl," he insisted, pointing to another girl in the picture that was standing in close proximity.

"She's cute!" I reassured him.

He settled back in his chair seemingly satisfied with my level of exuberance.

"We used to take funny pictures," he said in a sentimental tone. "She'd make a face or I'd make a face."

With child-like poise, he started to rapidly click through a series of pictures.

"This is one of my favorite pictures," he said. "We were at this bar and we were pretending like we were ringing each other's necks like an old married couple."

He stared at the picture with an irresistible fascination, like he had memorized every line in her face and was making sure each one was there.

"Just a couple of old married people," he said again.

He continued to stare at the picture under an enormous silence.

"We used to have a lot of fun," he said, his words trailing off after leaving his lips as if he was now in a faraway place.

He told me there had been an "incident" that later broke them up.

"I caught her with this other guy," he said with miserable eyes. "He was thirty-one. He didn't even go to Michigan, but he lived in a house on campus."

He paused, and suddenly picked up his coffee and took a sip.

"He actually used to date her roommate," he said half-heartedly. "Here—," his words trailed off again as he quickly pulled up a picture of Courtney's former roommate from her Facebook profile.

"She's cute," I said.

"Yeah, but not as cute as Courtney," he demanded, quickly pulling up other pictures on her Facebook profile as evidence.

He balanced his thoughts for a moment.

"This guy was the biggest loser," he said. "He was a bank teller and he was thirty-one. He lured her. While dating her roommate, he lured her."

He sat back in his chair.

"I didn't talk to her for three years," he said.

He went back to Courtney's Facebook profile and started clicking incessantly on pictures. A picture opened of Courtney with her sister and mother. He admired it for a moment with glassy eyes.

"She has a cool mother," he said. "Her mother's car was parked right outside my apartment on campus my senior year and she didn't know that Courtney and I weren't talking at the time and she saw me and said, 'Hello, Connor.'"

He paused for breath.

"Then I moved here for law school and one day, out of the blue, Courtney Facebooked me," he said. "She sent me this long message apologizing for everything. She said she was coming to Chicago and wanted to talk."

He hesitated as if he was momentarily in the throes of glory.

"We met up at 7 p.m. and we talked until 5 a.m. and we hashed out everything," he said. "Ten hours!"

He leaned forward confidentially.

"She sent me this afterward," he said, promptly pulling up a saved e-mail message from his phone that read: *"Connor...I'm glad we met up this weekend and talked for 10 HOURS! I will e-mail you this week when I'm not so busy/stressed at work. –C"*

He held the phone securely in the tender folds of the palm of his hand the entire time, letting me have only a privileged glimpse of the message as if his greatest fear was that I would take hold of it and accidentally press a wrong button and delete it.

After a moment or two, he pulled the phone back and safely pressed a button that exited out from it.

"We talk by e-mail all the time now like nothing ever happened," he said as if there was undoubtedly something funny about the whole thing.

On one brilliantly sunny Saturday morning, I met Gwynn at a small restaurant to study over breakfast. As I sat quietly staring down at my outline, she sat across from me practicing writing essay questions.

"We got our shots for the trip yesterday," she said during a short break. She had long planned a two week trip to South Africa with several friends following the bar exam.

"What kind of shots did you have to get?" I asked curiously.

"I had something like seven shots," she said.

"All in one arm?" I asked.

"Yeah, I got home and kind of crashed," she said, slowly crossing her long legs under the table. "The polio one kind of turns into a welt on your arm. Apparently, polio is spreading again in Africa and India and it is getting to the point where the CDC is considering putting it back on the list of vaccines only good for ten years."

She pushed her hair back from her eyes.

"They recommended that if you were going to eat anything local local—prepared locally—that you get the vaccine for dengue fever," she said.

She paused a moment.

"I had a couple of friends in the Peace Corps in the Dominican Republic and they've all had dengue fever," she said. "Apparently, you get hallucinations and because you are so dehydrated, you have to go to the hospital and they hook you up to an I.V. because you don't want to feel like you're going to die from being dehydrated."

She slowly smoothed down her hair.

"Apparently, everyone was getting it and it became a joke— it was like, 'Okay, it's your turn now,'" she said, smiling humorously.

I smiled back.

"So, I don't think I'm going to eat anything local prepared locally," she said, lifting her eyebrows to make a point. "Even though in the Philippines I did."

She leaned forward.

"In the Philippines, you'd walk along the markets and you'd see all these meats," she said, gesturing. "I'm adventurous with what I eat. There were several things I ate that I had no idea what I was eating. They spoke little English. You'd ask in Filipino, but, you know?"

She paused and sipped her coffee.

"There was this one fish that was in a leaf," she said. "I don't know what kind of fish it was—it was a fish sausage—but it was so good."

She pushed her hair back.

"I remember there was this one meat in a curry and when I tried it, it wasn't what I thought it was going to taste like," she said. "It was more gelatiny. But it was good. It was curried and it was in a leaf—again it was served in a leaf."

She smiled.

"I guess I'd eat anything in a leaf."

"I once saw this guy on TV eating scorpions in Vietnam," I remarked.

"See, I don't know if I would eat a scorpion," she said. "I think I draw the line at exoskeletons."

"Why do you draw the line there?" I asked.

"It's something about biting it and hearing the crunching of its bones," she said with a sort of grimace. "I don't think I would eat bugs. I don't think I would eat a grasshopper. This one guy was eating a grasshopper in the Philippines. I think I would have to be on a deserted island and be really hungry to eat a grasshopper."

That Sunday was Father's Day and there was a brunch planned at my parents' house and a card that had been bought and a gift that I had gone in on with Adam and Barbara, but my mother called early in the morning to tell me that everything had been called off because of one of my father's episodic stomach flare ups, which stemmed from his diverticulitis. When I called him in the afternoon to see how he was doing, he said he had eaten bland food all day, but felt better, and then he went on to talk to me for almost ten minutes about why I should buy a new electric shaver.

As it happens, my father has the tendency to repeat himself excruciatingly in conversations when attempting to make his point known as if the more times he says something the greater the chance I will hear it and see it his way. After we ceased talking about the electric shaver, he suggested that I call Ben Franks, a second cousin of his who was a partner at a big law firm.

"He may be able to give you some advice with the exam as well as how to talk to these firms and get a job," he said.

Worn-out from talking with my father, I only briefly spoke with my mother. Apparently, she had had her forty year high school anniversary the night before. In a talkative voice, she explained how everyone was the same age at the reunion.

"Well, everyone is typically the same age at a high school reunion," I said.

"Yeah, but everyone looked old," she said. "A few people recognized me right away without me having to say my name so that made me feel good."

That Monday, I met with Connor and Griffin at the coffee shop on State and Chestnut that had increasingly become our temporary curve of the world to write practice essay questions. Days had started to blend together in rather choppy sets and while the sun shined outside in dazzling glints of bright color hot to the eye, we studied at a dimly-lit table in an absurd crescendo of silence for seven conscientious hours.

As the day went on, I noticed from the corner of my eye Connor staring blankly out the window for prolonged periods of time as if he was responsible for wishing all the world's wishing.

At one point, during a short lunch break, Connor started revealing a hopeful plan he had recently conceived to help him lose weight in preparation for his trip to Madrid. No doubt it rested heavily on his mind. He said that he had signed up for a calorie counting website and that he had been religiously entering all the foods that he had consumed, the number of glasses of water he drank and the type and length of exercise he participated in for the past week.

"I have to enter it," he said evenly. "It keeps me honest."

In some excitement, we sat there as he pulled out his phone and logged onto the website.

"It's addictive," he said, searching for his profile. "I have it set at 1400 calories a day. That's my maximum."

Slight desperation inched across his face in perfect mutiny.

"If I exercise, it takes it into account," he added.

As he leaned forward, he told us that he had started to jog four miles each day, which burned 600 calories.

"The first day took me an hour and a half with all the starts and stops," he said. "But now it takes me thirty-five minutes." Sweat started to shine faintly from his temples.

"I'm only going to take Fridays off," he said.

He looked at his profile and entered a large coffee with milk and sugar, a plain bagel without cream cheese and, after searching for udon chicken soup without finding it, he regrettably settled for vegetable udon tempura soup, its closest match.

"It's more calories," he insisted. "The chicken that was in the soup was small pieces and it was baked. I'll just make a mental note."

On that Tuesday, I took a bus across the city and met Gibbs for lunch at a little downtown café on Monroe Street. I hadn't seen him since the rooftop party, which at the time seemed like a world away. Inside the café, it was exceedingly crowded with lounging bodies stuffed at small tables while a chorus of simultaneous voices blew in the air around us. We both ordered large sandwiches with sides of potato chips, which were ridged and crispy.

"How was Father's Day?" I asked, biting into my sandwich.

"Good," said Gibbs, adjusting his glasses. "We went up north to Ellen's parents' cottage."

As he took a bite of his sandwich, his eyes seemed a bit restless.

"My father has one up there too," he continued. "You should come sometime this summer. It's beautiful. It's peaceful. It's right on the lake and we have a pontoon boat."

"Great," I said. "How often do you go?"

"Every other weekend," he said. "Kara loves it up there. Usually, Ellen goes with her Friday morning and I'll drive up there Friday night or Saturday morning."

He drew a long breath.

"Listen to this," he said suddenly. "So we arrived there on Friday at nine and I'm hammered by ten. Ellen's dad makes these really strong Manhattans and I had four of them. And I didn't eat anything. Ellen's dad likes to drink."

He stared at me as if to make a point.

"It's something we have in common," he said, slightly shrugging his shoulders. "Ellen's family is totally dysfunctional, but this we have in common."

As his eyes roved about the restaurant, he wiped the sweat from his temples.

"Anyway, Ellen's dad passes out downstairs on the couch and, I don't know, drinking that much alcohol, maybe it was because I didn't eat anything, but I'm upstairs with Ellen in one of the guest bedrooms and, I don't know how, but I sleepwalked," he said, the last note emphasized in a high murmur, which followed the many murmurs and rhythms of the restaurant.

He paused a moment and watched for my reaction.

"I was sleepwalking into Ellen's mom's room and my arms are raised forward and I'm standing at the foot of her bed saying, 'I need to take the dishes out of the dishwasher,'" he said hilariously.

"Ellen's mom is like, 'Wake up! Wake up! Do you know what you're doing?' And I don't wake up fully. I'm like in this deep sleep, but I go back into the guest bedroom with Ellen," he said.

He turned his head side to side in embarrassment.

"The next morning, I go down for breakfast and Ellen's mom is like, 'Do you know what you did last night?'" he said. "And I couldn't remember. She's like, 'You were sleepwalking.'"

He gestured momentarily with his hands.

"And she told me what I said about the dishes," he said.

He took a bite of his sandwich.

"Later, I was talking with Ellen and I was like, 'You know how when I wake up in the morning after a few drinks sometimes I'm like, 'My pants are in a different place than where I put them?'" he said. "'Maybe I'm sleepwalking at night. Maybe I'm a sleepwalker at night and I don't even know it.'"

He tipped his head back and sipped his water.

"It's scary," he said. "I thought I was dreaming, but I guess a dream is only a dream if you are not awake."

I sat there quietly in thought. It sounded so profound. After a slight pause, he leaned forward with intense eyes.

"Have you talked to Becker lately?"

"No," I said, taking another bite.

"He's got it made," said Gibbs, lifting several chips toward his mouth. "I could live with some cushy position at a corporation without billables."

His voice seemed to hesitate as he settled his thoughts.

"I'll tell you, I don't know how long I will be able to do this. It's not just the politics or the yelling all the time. I know I have taken years off the end of my life from the stress. I probably took three years off the end of my life. I'm under this constant stress."

He took a deep breath.

"The first couple of weeks—I can't even explain," he said. "It was like a honeymoon. They treated me like I was a rising star. But the stress is mounting. They just keep giving me cases. I'm pushing paper. That's what Dick loves to say. We're pushing paper, moving cases. I'm a paper pusher. I'm Dick's paper pusher. Dick knows I am his soldier. I am his soldier. He just puts up with me. I know this."

"How serious are you about leaving?" I asked.

"It's this economy, I don't know," said Gibbs, taking his glasses off and gently wiping them with the soft edge of his napkin. "I just know I'm tired of the stomachache I get every morning. What will I get in trouble about today?"

He slipped his glasses back onto his face and adjusted them on his nose.

"You know, when we were at the cottage, I went with Ellen's dad one night to a bar and we drank with the locals," he said. He tipped his head back and sipped his water.

"Ellen's dad knows everybody," he said, leaning forward. "The District Attorney up there is retiring. He doesn't want to run again. He's like, 'Move out here now and in two years run for the D.A. The salary is a hundred grand. You try DUI cases, petty cases.'"

He looked at me for the first time with some excitement in his eyes.

"You try nothing cases, but its different there," he said. "It's a small town. I'm considering it because here I'm not being groomed for anything. I'm not working toward anything."

It was when June was at its warmest that I left work early with Jerry to go to the Cubs game one day. As the train thundered by in rackets of sound on the tracks outside Wrigley Field, I watched white clouds outlined in gold slowly float through an expanding blue sky as a yellow sun tinted the streets in a boyish sentimental glaze. There were beggars' shouts by vendors selling peanuts and herds of people in dense groups along Addison Street punctuated in the color blue marching toward the gates. In the air, the pleasant aroma of hot dogs drifted steamily in wind-swept throws.

Out on the field, the players were finishing batting practice in blinding brightness on the short cut grass while the wilderness of the ivy seemed to stretch lazily across the outfield walls in a green dream.

"Those hot dogs are the wrong ones," said Jerry, leisurely sitting back in the steam of the sun as a hot dog vendor passed by our row. "You gotta get the kosher ones with the grilled onions. They only sell them inside at the concession stands."

We stood up from our seats and rode the stairs near the gate's entrance down into the body of the ballpark where there was a curving line of gathered people.

"That's a bingo," he said, pointing to a stand where blackened hot dogs charred crisply on a grill beside a clump of darkening onions.

"I think I may get two," he said, getting gradually excited. "It's a guilty pleasure whenever I go to a game."

He wiped sweat from his forehead.

"I went spinning Tuesday and Wednesday," he said with a small gesture. "It's not a total justification, but it makes me feel better."

In the bottom of the third inning, the Cubs scored two runs to take a 2 to1 lead. As a huddled meeting ensued on the pitcher's mound, Jerry turned to me.

"Oh, by the way, I'm finally going to bring in that large sweets basket. The one from State Street Bakery."

"Yeah?" I said as if to show that I was deathly concerned with it.

"Friday," he said. "Friday is the day."

Jerry stared absently out at the field.

"It took a little while because I had a deposition seminar I had to attend, but it looks like Friday is the day," he said. "If I get the gift certificate by then."

In the fourth inning, the pitcher for the Reds bent over the mound holding his lower back in what appeared to be excruciating pain. 'Time' was immediately called by the home plate umpire as the trainer for the Reds ran swiftly out from the dugout under wild shouts from the crowd.

"He's had a bad back for most of the year," said Jerry, planting his elbows on each of the armrests. "I was reading about it this morning. It's been bothering him since spring training."

The trainer performed several examinations to check the pitcher's range of motion.

"I hurt my back once bowling," said Jerry. "It's the worst thing to hurt."

He turned toward me.

"I had been on a date. I was using a bowling ball that was too heavy. I was using a twenty-two pound ball. I don't know what I was thinking. I continued to bowl even though I had hurt it."

"Did you win?" I asked.

"Yeah, I won," he said. "I never went on another date with her though."

"You should have lost to her," I said.

"Yeah, I should have," he said. "I actually had to go to the chiropractor and get my back adjusted. It was really painful. Even years later, I sneezed so hard one time I had to go to the chiropractor to get it re-aligned again."

It was at that point the infamous beer vendor, who had married the woman Jerry shared his tickets with, walked down our section. Jerry stood to get his attention and formally introduced us. The beer vendor, who had matted down hair under a blue visor and sweat slowly dripping from his forehead, stood at ease. As we shook hands, I told him I would take two beers.

"I don't drink," Jerry broke in. "You better just get one."

As the beer vendor cracked open a can of beer, Jerry leaned forward and whispered to him, "I told him all about you and Margaret."

"Oh, yeah?" said the beer vendor, surprised about his notoriety.

"It's a fairy tale," said Jerry. "It's a fairy tale if I've ever seen one."

After the beer vendor had left, I asked Jerry if he had ever been married.

"No," he said, looking a bit sun-flushed. "Never married. I guess I just haven't met *my* Margaret yet."

After a short pause, Jerry started to tell me about his last girlfriend though he didn't tell me how long ago it was.

"We were both Harry Potter fans and I've read all of them, but she had only read the first four so I lent her the last three," said Jerry, joining his hands together. "We went out a handful of times and then one day she just stopped returning my calls. I'd e-mail her and I'd know she read them because I could check its status, but she never replied."

He turned his head out to the field.

"She kept the books," he said in a pitying voice.

He turned back toward me.

"She never gave them back. I e-mailed her about it one time and again she read it, but never replied. I had to buy the last three again so I would have a complete collection. You'd think she would just say something like, 'I'll ship them to you,' or something."

As Jerry wiped his face of sweat with a napkin, he started to tell me about his last date, which he said was "several weeks ago."

"We met at a seminar and she's an actress and she invited me to her show. I took her out for a drink afterward. I called her the next day, but she never called me back."

He hesitated.

"It's all right though," he began again. "As an actress, she may not be the most careful person. Not being in the professional world, her turnaround time in getting back to people may be different. So she still may call."

That night I met Gwynn along Lakeshore Drive for a walk. It was Chicago's little Garden of Eden and outside the gates of Oak Street Beach there was well kept shrubbery, newly planted flowers, perfectly trimmed hedges, and neat green lawns. There was a faint breeze swaying treetops, and as the heat drew down and stole the night air, the coolness from the lake still made it pleasant.

Across the luminous blue sky the first stars began to sparkle, and as we walked under the viaduct at Oak Street to the beach, which stood between Lakeshore Drive and Lake Michigan, I watched the tops of the early 20th Century buildings fall off from sight. On the other side, I looked back across the traffic, and the buildings, now standing at attention, seemed to be looking at the water like a jury with the John Hancock Building a block down as the foreman.

The shore was filled with people walking and jogging and riding bicycles. We strolled along the edge of the beach proper while the open lake, dark against the light, shimmered in the endless beyond. There was a slight tide and a ripple in the water near its edge. Out on the horizon, the early moon shined an arc of light across the sky and as the night darkened, we started to realize we were more and more by ourselves. I looked up and saw the blinking lights on the spires above the John Hancock Building and they were like eyes in the sky joining the stars and suddenly we weren't alone.

The curve of the shore along Oak Street Beach came to an unseen tip in the distance as the blaze of the Ferris wheel at Navy Pier shined patterns of light in the fading twilight air. As the traffic passed in sound along Lakeshore Drive, volleyball games on the beach started to come to an end and people dripping with water sauntered out of the lake and to the sand to pick up their towels and dry off. To our right, near the water's edge, a man crouching like a baseball catcher cupped his hands as his wife poured water from a plastic water bottle into them for two little twin poodles to slurp with thirsty tongues while the wind blew through their white fluffy fur.

We spotted boats on the lake and talked for a little while about the economy.

"If anyone asks me whether I am interviewing with anyone just once more I don't know what I'm gonna do," said Gwynn as we idled along the lakefront. "I can't believe I'm graduating in this market."

She turned toward me.

"One of the professors told me last week that he feels bad teaching with the way the economy is now. 'What's the point?' he said. 'Kids aren't getting jobs.' You never hear faculty talk that way. He did."

The wind gently swept through her hair in a stunningly perfect way as her earrings slowly danced in the moonlight.

"I remember my grandmother telling me about the Great Depression and how she used to take home extra sugar packets from the restaurants," she added ominously.

Down by the water, there was a film crew near the beach at Ohio Street—a comedian I knew of from *Saturday Night Live* was there, dressed in a black shirt and black pants filming bumpers introducing segments for a TV comedy special that was going to air later in the summer. People gathered around the edge of the walk and watched the filming against the lowered sky.

"No flash photography," said a crew member holding a clipboard.

"Flashing is all right, but no flash photography," said the comedian without breaking a serious face.

The early evening air was suddenly fresh and as Gwynn reached for my hand I realized that it was the first time we had held hands.

"Excuse me, sir, but can you tell me the time?" asked a woman pushing a carriage with a small sleeping child. Her husband stood a few steps behind, waiting.

"It's eight-thirty," I said glancing at my watch.

"Thank you," she said.

After a slight hesitation, I turned to Gwynn.

"I guess I am now officially a 'sir,'" I said as a pained thought of getting older crept across my face.

Gwynn stared at me for a moment and smiled.

"Well, I would be called 'Miss' or 'Ms.,'" she said.

"Or Mademoiselle," I said.

"Ah, if we were in France, yes," she said.

As we teetered along the widening base of the shore, we came to a long stretch of outlying lights around Buckingham Fountain. Gwynn's face was very close to mine and as I pulled her closer, we kissed in a quiet moment under the bright glitter of the stars.

One sunny afternoon, Griffin decided to take the day off from studying and go for a boat ride on the lake along the gleaming skyline in his father's boat, which was docked at Monroe Harbor, and I met up with Connor at the coffee shop alone. Connor was already there sitting at a table against the shaded windows on the far side of the shop in a solitary darkened slouch amid other sparsely darkened figures when I arrived. I sat down in the chair opposite him at the table and began to set forth my books. As he looked up at me, he started to tell me in an excited voice about how he had been following the soccer match between Spain and the U.S. on his laptop all morning.

"When the U.S. scored their second goal, I yelled so loud everyone kind of turned their head and looked at me," he said, smiling.

We spoke more about the soccer match, and then he began to tell me about his childhood and how he never played soccer, but had always been an avid fan.

"My father played a lot of soccer when he was younger, but he thinks there is too much emphasis on sports in America," he explained.

"So he de-emphasized it," I said.

"Yeah, he emphasized academics instead," he said, lightly tapping the table with his knuckles.

It was at that point his phone vibrated. His eyes narrowed as he quieted and read the message.

The next morning it rained early and for awhile it seemed endless. There were loud claps of thunder and bright flashes of lightning across a silver sky as heavy sheets of slanted rain fell to the earth. I trudged to work through a maze of rain blown streets and hung up my dripping coat on a hook in my office. Suddenly, across the hallway, I heard a mysterious woman's voice coming from Jerry's office.

As I went over, I saw Jerry through the doorway sitting still at his desk donning a serene face while speaking with an attractive woman I had never seen before. I looked once more at them and then leaned against the wall without a sound and curiously listened for a moment longer.

"Hilde?" he said with a pause. "Do you speak German?"

"No," said Hilde, who was sitting in the chair opposite Jerry's desk. "Do you?"

"Mein Name ist Jerry," he said excitedly.

She smiled sort of awkwardly.

"I went to Austria and I spoke German there the entire time," said Jerry. "You have a slight accent. When did you come to the states?"

"Five years ago," said Hilde.

"Only five years ago?" said Jerry. "You're accent is so slight I would bet money you knew English for a long time."

"Well, I studied it in high school," said Hilde.

Jerry sat there listening with great interest.

"It's very slight," said Jerry. "Now, ah, what activities do you like to do?"

"I used to be involved in synchronized swimming," said Hilde. "I was in the French Club in high school. I travel a lot. I spent a semester in Russia during college."

"Did you know I was a Russian History major in college?" asked Jerry.

"No," said Hilde. "I did not."

"Yeah," said Jerry.

"What periods did you study?" asked Hilde.

"All," said Jerry. "All of them; Catherine the Great, Peter the Great, Ivan the Terrible. There were a lot of good periods and a lot of bad periods."

She nodded with faint interest.

"She likes spinning and I like spinning," said Jerry the next morning as he recounted in intricate detail his meeting with Hilde, who he had apparently met on the internet. He then told me in a sort of delight that had washed slowly over his face that he had asked her out to a Cubs game.

"If the Cubs game goes well, I'm going to ask her if she wants to come to my gym as a guest and go to a spinning class with me," he said, clearing his throat. "The only problem is that after those classes I'm usually drenched in sweat."

"So when are you going to the game?" I asked.

"I sent her an e-mail asking her which game she wanted to go to—tomorrow or Thursday—and she responded: 'Yes.' So, I don't know which one. And I haven't been able to get a hold of her since."

"So what are you going to do?" I asked.

"I don't know," he said. "I don't want her to go tomorrow and think I stood her up. It sounds silly, but I may have to go to both games, that is, if she doesn't show up tomorrow and given I still can't get a hold of her."

For the rest of the day, Jerry remained hopeful. It was only later in the week that I learned he had spent both evenings alone waiting outside the front gates at Wrigley Field under a dreamy sky of bright falling stars hoping she would come. But she never did.

"How much weight have you lost?" I asked Connor one afternoon at our usual table by the window at the coffee shop. It was a pointed question that I had wanted to ask him for nearly a week because it seemed like he had dropped a considerable amount of weight.

"What?" he murmured in burnt coffee fumes as if it was a source of satisfaction.

"I can tell," I said. "You look thinner. I can see it in your face."

"I'm down eleven pounds," he said, finally. "I'm 188."

"You really like Courtney," I said.

"She's the gold standard," he said flatly.

He began to talk eagerly.

"She's cute, she's smart, and she's funny. She's like the top ten percent."

"Are you saying ninety percent of the world is not cute?" I asked.

"Yes," he said automatically. "Maybe eighty-five percent. What do you think the percentage is?"

"Um," I stumbled.

"Seventy percent," he broke in.

After a slight pause, he started to tell me about how he found out recently that Courtney had a new boyfriend.

"Don't you think this guy is in less of a position than her?" he asked, sitting back against his chair.

"Why do you say that?" I asked.

"Because she's in demand," he said. "She has something that people want."

"Which is what?" I asked.

"Being in a relationship with her," he said in a rising voice.

There was a silence.

"Does she have any siblings?" I asked.

"She has a sister," he said. "Her sister is prettier, but she is evil."

"Evil?" I asked. "Like how?"

"Their relationship is rooted in hate," he said. "Her sister will say things like, 'I went to Northwestern. You're such a loser, blah, blah, blah for going to Michigan.'"

He hesitated for a moment and then exclaimed, "She's an awful person."

"The sister is younger, right?" I asked.

"Yeah," he said.

"She's at Northwestern Law School?" I asked.

"No, she went there for undergrad," he said. "She's already out. She works at ABC News."

"So you're friend is the oldest?" I asked.

"Yeah," he said.

"Are there others?" I asked.

"She has two younger brothers," he said, gesturing. "One is a senior in high school and the other is at Dartmouth. And she has two half-brothers that are younger. They're like in grade school.

Her parents are divorced. Her father did the typical mid-life crisis thing and cheated on his wife then married a trophy wife."

He looked down and checked his phone.

"Her mother married this Japanese guy," he began again. "He doesn't even speak English. My friend has never said anything, but I know why she married him," he added, gesturing with his fingers to symbolize money. "It's not unheard of. She was in a weaker financial position."

"So why is your friend with this new guy?" I asked. "How did they meet?"

"Law school," he said. "He's younger than her. He's twenty-four. She's twenty-six. I don't get it. She usually goes for guys much older."

"Like her boss," I said.

He looked at me, knowingly. He had told me earlier that her boss, who was married and had two children, had come on to her the previous summer.

"Yeah, but she hasn't seen him in a long time," he said, his words trailing off. "She hasn't seen him since last summer. I think she's probably lonely. He's probably a default boyfriend."

He drew his coffee to his mouth and sipped.

"How much power do you have in a relationship if you're a default boyfriend?" he muttered.

He paused, suddenly glancing about the coffee shop.

"Look, girls know when they're cute," he said. "You don't have to tell them. All they need to do is look in the mirror. I have one friend out in New York, an attorney. She moved out there after the school year to take the bar. She doesn't have a job. I was like, 'How are you going to get a job there in this market?' And she's like, 'I'll wink and I'll smile.' She's a pretty girl. Whether that works despite her poor grades is yet to be seen."

There was a short pause.

"I have another friend here, in Chicago, who is borderline cute and she is very insecure," he said. "She goes out with all of these guys and they sleep with her and then later she's like, 'I don't know why they don't want to talk to me anymore.' She's like, 'I can't find any nice guys.'"

He stared at me as if to make a point.

"It's because she's insecure," he said. "She goes out with all these dumb frat guys. She doesn't understand they only wanted to bed her, they had no interest in being in a relationship with her or marrying her."

"Do you think she goes out with them because she thinks they're handsome or because she thinks they think she is cute?" I asked.

"I think more the latter," he said in a thoughtful pause. "You don't know this girl. She is so superficial. I saw her high school yearbook picture once and she looked so anorexic. She had to be treated."

"What would you rate Courtney on looks on a scale of one to ten?" I asked.

"Seven," he said. "She's cute."

"Your friend in New York?" I asked.

"Eight," he said. "She's pretty."

"Your friend in Chicago?" I asked.

"A six," he said. "She's kinda cute. She's borderline cute." He relaxed a little.

"The funny thing is that Courtney doesn't see the irony in what she did with her married boss in comparison with what her dad did to her mom," he said.

"Do you know this is the first girl that doesn't know all of my friends?" asked Griffin one day on the bus ride back from class. He was telling me about the bridesmaid he had met at his cousin's wedding in L.A. back in the spring. She apparently now had a name and it was Blair.

"It's kind of cool," he said. "And it's good if we break-up because then you don't have the 'whose friend is with who' thing going on."

"You've been seeing a lot of each other recently," I said.

"Yeah," he said.

He lowered his voice.

"Listen, we're going to this D.J. thing at The Stage tonight. I asked her two weeks ago not knowing it was her birthday."

"What D.J. thing?" I asked.

"Well, it's these D.J.'s and they play against one another," he said, gesturing. "It's not techno or anything like that."

"It's tough to have a birthday the first few weeks," I said.

"Yeah," he said. "I wasn't going to do much. I was just going to do this D.J. thing, but now I have other friends that are like, 'You got to take her to dinner.' And so, well, we've been hanging out a lot recently so I think I have to take her to dinner beforehand. I made reservations at this place called Milo's. Have you ever been there?"

"No," I said.

"It's like my favorite restaurant," said Griffin. "It's Italian." He hesitated.

"Do you think I need to get her flowers or a present?" he asked.

"You've been seeing her three or four weeks?" I said, pausing in thought. "I think you can get her flowers or a small present. Either or."

"But then it's like she can't take it with her," he said as if he was expecting me to say that.

"Is she girlfriend status?" I asked. "Like would you refer to her as your girlfriend when introducing her?"

"No," he said, slightly turning his head. "I don't think I've ever referred to any girl I dated as my girlfriend. I think that would freak me out. Even the girl that I dated for two years in college I don't think I ever referred to her as my girlfriend."

"How would you introduce her?" I asked.

"I'm just going to say her name," he said. "I'm going to say, 'This is Blair.'"

The next day, the sun shined high in the east, bathing the city in serene flames of bright yellow light. At twelve-thirty, I met Connor at a small Mediterranean restaurant and we jotted down answers to several essay questions over lunch. Supposedly, Griffin wanted to study on his deck that afternoon while listening to the Cubs game.

"That's a lot of hummus," I said, looking at the huge mound of it piled on the side of his plate.

"Have you ever seen a fat person eating hummus for every meal?" asked Connor, pulling his chair closer to the table. "It's only like three hundred calories for an entire container."

"Have you heard from your sister?" I asked.

Connor had decided to apply to a Masters in Taxation program and had sent his personal essay for his application to his sister in New York to edit.

"All right, so my sister was in London on a trip," he started, "and, as you know, she's supposed to edit it, but because she's traveling, I have to ask her how the trip is and all that filler crap in my e-mail before I can ask her about my paper and so at the end I say, 'By the way, have you had a chance to edit my paper, blah, blah, blah.' And so she e-mails me back and tells me all about her trip, but doesn't say anything about my essay."

He dipped pita into his hummus and brought it forward to his mouth.

"The next day, I e-mailed her back and said, 'Are you going to edit my essay or not?'" he said, chewing. "But now she's in Paris and she writes back, 'Let me get settled for a couple of weeks—I just got here.'"

"A couple of weeks?" I asked.

"Well, she's going to be there for a year," he said, reaching toward the pita.

At that moment, a man that stood about five-six wearing khaki shorts and brown sandals entered the restaurant. Connor paused, examining him from head to foot.

"I told you my rule about who should take their shirt off at the beach, right?" he asked.

"Right," I said.

"Well, I have another rule," he said. "Short people shouldn't wear shorts."

"Why?" I asked somewhat amused.

"Because I think it looks bad," he said. "I don't own any."

"So you're not taking shorts with you to Madrid?" I asked. "It's going to be in the high eighties there."

"No," he said.

"What are you going to wear?" I asked.

"Jeans," he said.

"What are you going to wear on the beach?" I asked.

"My Michigan athletic shorts," he said. "Athletic shorts are okay when you're running or if you're on the beach."

"Can you use them as a swimsuit?" I asked.

"I'm not going swimming," he said.

"You're not going swimming?" I asked.

"I can't swim," he said.

A moment later his phone vibrated in tiny echoes along the table. He quickly grabbed it and bent forward to read the message. For the next three minutes, he sat there in a prolonged silence typing a response. I looked out the window at the people passing on the street thinking about all the things one could do if you could just bottle the amount of time he spent on his phone, and when I looked back at him I noticed a stream of blood trickling from his nose.

"Your nose is bleeding," I said, gesturing.

"What?" he asked distracted.

"Your nose!" I pointed. "It's bleeding."

Almost without looking away from his phone, he quickly reached for a napkin from the table and pinched his nose with it. He then looked up at me.

"I have a thin, tiny vein right on the edge of my left inner nostril," he said muffled under the napkin as he tipped his head back to a forty-five degree angle. "As a result I often get nosebleeds."

As I sat there, I watched as he attempted to continue to type into his phone with one hand while pinching his nose with the other.

184. 183. 182. As the end of June baked the city with heat, Connor kept losing more and more weight. One afternoon, I was standing at the crosswalk by State and Erie in the hot sun and I saw him come from behind me in a sweaty blur and run right through the intersection and I shouted after him, but he had his headphones on and didn't hear me. Dodging pedestrians loping on the other side of the street, he continued running, carrying the exuberant hopefulness that all young men need to fuel their dreams.

On the last Saturday before July, I took the 151 bus to Union Station to catch a train to the suburbs for a belated Father's Day celebration at my parents' house. As soon as I walked inside the front door of the house, I heard a little, excited voice shout "I'm here! I'm upstairs!" It was the voice of my five-year-old niece, Lilly.

"Where are you Lilly?" I shouted.

"I'm in the playroom," she answered.

"Come downstairs and give me a hug," I said.

She rushed down the stairs and gave me a semi-hug with her shoulders.

"Use your arms, Lilly," I said.

She often had to be reminded to use her arms when giving hugs.

"Uncle Thomas?" she started.

I bent forward, listening.

"Yes?"

"Is today Sunday?" she asked.

"No, it's Saturday," I said.

"We usually get together at nana's house on Sunday," she said.

"Well, we're doing it today as well to make-up for Father's Day," I said. "Remember a couple of weeks ago when papa wasn't feeling well?"

She nodded slightly.

"We were supposed to celebrate it then," I said.

"Lilly, come to the dinner table," said Susan, my sister-in-law, from the kitchen.

"Pancakes!" shouted Lilly in excitement. "Pancakes!"

Apparently, we were going to have pancakes and eggs for dinner just for "something different."

Lilly rushed into the empty dining room. A moment or two later, everyone started to sit down at the table and I went around with a water pitcher pouring water into empty glasses.

"Lilly, on a scale from one to ten, if ten is your favorite and one is your least favorite, where would you rank pancakes?" I asked.

"Ah, two?" she said, leaning forward with enthusiasm.

"I thought they were your favorite," I said.

"Um, five?" she said, looking for my approval.

"All right," I said.

"Adam, would you come downstairs with a couple of toys for Nellie?" shouted Susan from the dinner table up the stairs. "Dinner's ready!"

"Oh, and Adam, can you wake up dad?" shouted my mother. "He was taking a short nap."

Adam came down with Scott, who was my two-year-old nephew.

"Oh, I forgot the toys for Nellie," said Adam as he exchanged a short glance with Susan.

"Daddy! Daddy! Did you wake up papa?" asked Lilly.

"Which toys should I get?" asked Adam, unwavering from his glance.

"One of the stuffed animals," said Susan.

Adam nodded and started backing up into the foyer.

"Daddy!" said Lilly in an overdramatic sigh to get his attention. "Did you wake up papa?"

"No, am I supposed to?" asked Adam as he looked down at her.

"Yes," shouted Susan from the dining room in confirmation.

"I think yes," said Lilly.

Adam shuffled up the stairs and came down a moment later.

"Hey, mom, I remember when I was a boy I used to love this tiny, little Snoopy," said Adam, holding the Snoopy in the air. "Do you remember this Snoopy?"

"A huh," said my mother, distracted. She was in the middle of placing a glass tray with scrambled egg whites on the table. "All right, this is hot."

"You want a little syrup?" Susan asked Lilly, who stacked two pancakes onto her plate.

"Ah, yes," said Lilly under little movements.

"Who wants some eggs?" asked Adam.

"Adam, hello," said my father as he walked into the kitchen.

"I was just going to get you," said Adam.

"Oh, breakfast time," said my father as he peaked his head into the dining room.

"And we have French toast," said my mother, rushing back into the kitchen.

My father took some eggs and three pancakes.

"Eileen? Where's the French toast?" asked my father, not having heard her earlier.

"It's coming," my mother said. "It's coming. It will be out in one minute."

"One minute?" he said. "Why didn't you make it earlier?"

"It's just heating up," she said.

"We're going to have eggs and pancakes," Adam said to Scott.

"No," cried Scott in a whiny, soft-sounding voice.

"Where's Barbara?" asked my father.

"She's running a little late," said my mother. "She will be here in five minutes."

"By the way, the French toast is very good," my father said to Susan.

Susan nodded.

"Oh, we have French toast?" asked Adam, noticing the French toast for the first time. "Susan, did you see we have French toast?"

Susan nodded.

"I have scalloped apples too," my mother said, hurrying into the kitchen to get the just mentioned platter of scalloped apples.

"Eileen, will you sit down at the table?" asked my father. "You remind me of my mother. People used to laugh at her. We have enough food for the entire neighborhood."

"I'm coming," said my mother from the kitchen.

"Tom, I spoke with Ben Franks on the phone yesterday and he would like to meet with you," said my father. "He's been through everything you're going through. He's a very bright guy and he can tell you how to approach getting a job. You've got to start networking."

I nodded with a mouthful of pancake.

"He gave me his cell phone number—call him," he said, handing me a folded piece of paper. "You can't be afraid to do these things. I know you have the exam, but call him. Otherwise you're going to find yourself without a job after the exam."

Across the table, Lilly started making funny faces at me as she chewed little forkfuls of her pancake.

"Lilly, today is backwards," I said. "We're going to have breakfast for dinner and dinner for breakfast. Is that correct?"

"No," she said. "We're going to have breakfast for dinner and dinner for dessert."

"Lilly," Adam broke in, "you're going to have breakfast for breakfast tomorrow." He looked at her reassuringly as she sat there thinking.

That Monday, Jerry slowly went around the office to personally notify each law clerk about a departmental meeting he had scheduled in the conference room, which would "review several procedural changes."

"Not this Thursday, but next Thursday," he said importantly. "Did you get the e-mail?"

"I haven't checked yet," I said.

"All right, well, I just sent it, so I just wanted you to know," he said, his face sinking slightly. "I don't even know if I have everybody's correct e-mail address. Like, for instance, they spelled Amanda's last name wrong in the system so she never got the e-mail."

"I'll check," I said.

"Good," he said. "Oh, by the way, we should be getting that sweets basket for the meeting. I apologize for the delay. I didn't get the gift certificate until last week. They actually had to send it to me in the mail."

As he slunk off to the next office, I could hear him tell Jenny, a clerk, the exact same thing he had just explained to me.

Later, I listened as he broke out into a rendition of the *Major-General's Song* from Gilbert and Sullivan's *Pirates of Penzance* when he overheard Dana, another clerk, telling someone that she was going to see the play that weekend at one of the local colleges.

"I'm a Gilbert and Sullivan nut," said Jerry proudly afterward.

It was at that point he proceeded to sing more of the *Major-General's Song*.

"I've probably seen *Pirates of Penzance* fifty times over the years," he confessed excitedly.

As I watched Jerry that day, deep down inside, it occurred to me that he would have gone around to each clerk and personally explained his e-mail even if he knew everyone had received it because I think he was lonely and was sitting alone behind his wide, oak desk in his nice, big, corner office with his conversational magnets and Cubs coffee mug and he had been doing so all afternoon.

That Thursday, I met with Ben Franks at his office on Wacker and Monroe. His firm was on the twenty-second floor and while I waited in the cool lobby watching the news headlines flash on a flat screen, I looked out at the incredible views of the city below.

"Tom, how are you?" asked Ben, walking into the lobby. He was wearing a dark, undoubtedly expensive suit, and crisp yellow tie.

I stood up and walked over to him.

"Good," I said.

We shook hands.

"I just want to thank you, Ben," I said.

"For what?" he asked.

"For taking your time and meeting with me," I said.

"Please," he said. "Of course."

I followed him down a long wood-paneled hallway lined with plush carpeting to his office at the far end. The views of the city from inside his office were even more incredible than in the lobby. I looked about his office as he shut the door behind me.

"Come," he gestured to the chair opposite his desk, "have a seat."

I walked over and sat down. He stepped forward and sat down in the chair behind his desk.

"So I hear you're studying for the bar exam," he said.

"Yes," I said.

"Well, let's start off by me telling you a little about myself," he said. "And then we can talk about what you're looking for job-wise."

"All right," I said.

"I remember taking the bar exam," he said. "It was—could it be forty years ago?"

He leaned forward slightly.

"Yes," he said. "It was forty years ago. Imagine that."

He paused in thought.

"Anyway, I've been practicing for a long time," he said. "I get paid what I am paid because of this," he added, gesturing to his gray hair.

"Now, some of my Associates are like, 'Ben, why do you still do it?'" he said.

He looked at me closely.

"And you know what?" he said. "I don't think I would ever go into a profession again where you sell your time. If you are in business, you are selling an item. You can hire sales people or a sales manager to handle sales. You could be in the fucking Bahamas and someone could go onto your website and fucking point and click on your item and buy it."

His eyes moved gradually around the office.

"As an attorney, you sell your time," he said. "You have to actually be there and grind out the hour. Make the buck yourself. And there's no coasting. You just grind it."

His eyes rested on me.

"I have clients, guys I've known for years and they're like, 'Ben, we want you to do it,'" he said. "My billing rate is, you know," he said, gesturing with his hand high in the air, "and I'm like, 'You don't need me to do it. I can farm it to an Associate.' And they're like, 'Ben, we want you to do it.'"

He studied my reaction.

"It's funny," he said. "It's like everything in my life is down to the exact minute. My wife, you know Terri, she asks me how long it will take me at the grocery store after work."

He locked his fingers together.

"With billable hours, every hour is divided by .10," he said. "Every six minutes I bill .01 of an hour. It's a crazy way to sell yourself. When I'm at the gym, I find myself saying, 'That was .05 of an hour,' like a real freak. The other day, our neighbors came over. Their daughter is in school with my granddaughter Diana and we all worked on a project for school. Our neighbor happens to be Michael Weir. Michael is a corporate attorney with Kinder Perkins and we were laughing after finishing the project. It took two and a half hours to do it. We were saying this had to be the most expensive school project in the history of mankind, you know?"

He glanced toward the skyline through his window and then looked over at me.

"I remember when I was twenty-five," he said. "No client comes to you when you're twenty-five. It's like when you are looking for a doctor. You don't want the new one that just graduated. You don't want the very old one, the one shaking, the one twenty years past his prime. You want the seasoned one who has done it so many times he can do it in his sleep though. Same thing with attorneys."

"How did you get your first job?" I asked.

"I happened to do very well in law school," he said, unlocking his fingers and settling back in his chair. "But luck plays into everything. I really made my mark when I went to a childhood friend's shiva for his mom."

He paused a moment.

"I see my friend and tell him, 'I'm really sorry about your mom,'" he said. "Well, one of my clients is there and I have this man approach me and he is the founder of this business, it's a multi-million dollar business, and he says, 'I've heard some great things about you,' pointing with his head toward my client. They never had proper legal representation and we start talking and he's my client for the next twenty years. A shiva! True story. Sometimes it's just luck."

The next day, the unclouded sky painted itself a profound powder blue as bright yellow sun splashes danced in front of my eyes on the walk to the coffee shop in a summer waltz of sorts with my own moving shadow. With Connor's mother in town for the day, I met Griffin alone. We studied quietly at a table near the counter for eight hours with lowered heads and eyes fastened on tiny endless print. The last four hours had been, in turn, boring and tiring. I went up to the counter to get another coffee around four o'clock. The coffee was slightly bitter and though a little sugar made it sweeter, it was still bitter going down. When I returned to the table, Griffin started talking about Blair and how he was worried that it was getting too serious between the two of them too fast.

"What's my out?" he asked in a voice dropping into a confidential tone.

"What do you mean?" I asked.

"It's getting serious," he said. "I don't want to break-up with her, but what if I did?"

"How long has it been?" I asked.

"Five weeks," he said.

"That's a long time," I said.

"A huh," he murmured.

"You don't need an out," I suggested. "You just say it's getting too serious and you're not ready for something serious. I had a friend that went out with this girl for eight years and one day he told her it wasn't what he wanted anymore."

There was a pause.

"It happens," I said.

"I don't see there being any way out of it right now without a lot of crying," he said.

"But you don't want to break-up," I said.

"Right," he said.

"And so it's not her, it's that you have some commitment issues," I said.

"Well, yeah," he said, propping his elbows on the table. "Don't you ever think, 'How am I going to get out of this if I want to?'"

"So you just want an excuse to put away in your back pocket to use if you want to?" I asked.

"Yeah," he said with a slight nod.

After a short silence, he changed subjects and asked whether I was keeping pace with the bar study schedule. He then told me of an idea he had been entertaining for the last day or two.

"It's a little out there, it's a little crazy, but do you think it would be a good idea to just get on a train or something and head west?" he asked.

I looked at him cautiously.

"No distractions, no roommate watching *Nights at Rodanthe* with his girlfriend for the fifteenth time, no telephone, no television," he said, pressing his palms together.

As he went on, I realized he was actually being serious.

"You would just study on the train?" I asked.

"Yeah," said Griffin, his voice slightly cracking. "Like a week before the exam. Nothing but passing scenery. No distractions."

"Seriously?" I asked.

"I'd take it to like Seattle," he said, gesturing. "And when I got there I'd ask, 'When's the next train to Chicago? Twelve hours? All right.'"

"I don't know," I said, after a slight hesitation. "I don't think it's a good idea. If you want to do it, do something like that now, not a week before the exam."

At six o'clock, Griffin packed up his books for the night and left, and for awhile everything became very still and quiet around me. At seven-thirty, Gwynn called and said that she was down the street with Mitchell and asked if I wanted to come outside for a short break to meet him. I walked outside just as they were crossing at the intersection. Gwynn waved with her flashcards in her hand.

"Hi, Mitchell," I said, bending down to pet his head.

"Mitchell, this is Tom," said Gwynn in a formal way.

At that exact moment, a butterfly fluttered in the air taking Mitchell's attention with it.

"He seems way more interested in the butterfly," said Gwynn, laughing. "I apologize."

Mitchell started to bark at the butterfly.

"I swear he has A.D.D.," she said. "You might want to know that he has O.C.D. too. Whenever we go for a walk, I have to clean his feet or he sits there and cleans them himself obsessively. When it gets cold outside I put little booties on him, but because he won't wear his shoes we only walk far enough in the snow for him to do his business."

The wind massaged Mitchell's fur as I pet his head.

"How's studying going today?" I asked.

"Today is knife wound and stitches in the thigh day," she said, balancing a smile. "It's an improvement. Yesterday was forehead gash and severed thumb day. Tomorrow? Who knows what tomorrow will bring."

Gwynn turned to Mitchell.

"Mitchell, this is Tom."

Mitchell still seemed captivated by the effortlessness of the butterfly fluttering in the air.

"Oh well," she said as we smiled at each other. "Anyway, so we have that simulated MBE on the sixth, right?"

"Right," I said.

"Well, I just found out that my parents are coming to town for the fourth after all and this is after that whole back and forth from last week," she said. "I was like, 'Are you sure you want to come in on the fourth? You know that I'm studying. I hope you're not expecting me to hang out other than during the dinners you are going to be paying for.'"

About forty-five minutes north of the city was a small town along the lake called Country Lakes. It was there along a sleepy stretch of waterfront property by a pier and a beach where Gibbs had his summer cottage. It was because of this that Griffin and I drove up there for the July 4th weekend.

There was the usual heavy morning traffic in the city limits, but as we made our way out from the arching call of Chicagoland's reach, there were only bunches of cars on the highway and then the sweep of open roads of the country. Across the sky there was a deep light blue with white billowy clouds and a brilliant yellow sun in a canvas of color. The green blur in the passing landscape hinted of summer trees while every couple of miles there were roadside signs advertising fireworks blowout sales.

As we turned into Country Lakes, we drove along a winding road—a Main Street—with little shops and restaurants and a bakery on the corner. We took a right at a sign that said "Bait Shop: minnows, tackle and worms." The cottage was at the end of the street, set back from the road and partially hidden by a great oak tree. As we pulled up to the walk in the front, Ellen Gibbs was standing in a floral summer dress on the front lawn near a flower garden with Kara blowing bubbles into the air.

"Bubbles," shouted Kara, joyously, trying to catch one.

"Oh, you almost got one," said Ellen.

I had met Ellen once before at the Barrister's Ball at the InterContinental Hotel during my second year of law school. I remembered that she had told me her father was a former vice president of an airline and that they could fly anywhere in the world for free if they waited standby, and though she went through all the places she wanted to go, she had said she never had the time to actually go anywhere.

As I watched Kara run after a bubble drifting just out of her reach and fall safely into the cushion of a thousand green blades of grass in the neatly cut lawn, Ellen greeted us cheerfully and we talked for several minutes.

"This is actually Jim's parent's cottage, but they're in Rome for two weeks," she said. "My father has one up the road. This is where we first met. We saw each other every summer."

She bent down and dipped a stick into the rim of a small bottle washing over with soapy liquid and blew a sky full of floating bubbles, which sent Kara floating in excitement right after them in shaky hobbles.

"It was Kara's second birthday yesterday, but we were so busy with getting ready for the weekend that we just didn't tell her it was her birthday," she said quietly. "We decided we would just celebrate it tonight if nobody minds."

"Sure," I said.

"We were going to celebrate it next week with Jim's step-father, John, who just turned sixty-five, but my mother-in-law said she'd rather separate the two birthdays to be fair to John," she said, as if there had been some brooding inner frustration.

"No problem," said Griffin.

Ellen smiled.

"Come on, let's find Jim," she said, turning to pick Kara up in her arms. "He's out back."

We walked up the gravel bend to the front door of the cottage. Inside, a narrow hallway led to the kitchen. Bright natural sunlight shined in broad yellow streaks through glass windows on either side as the lake swept fresh air through the half-open window over the sink, moving a wind chime to dangle in delight. On the refrigerator, there were pictures of the three of them looking happy out on the lake.

After picking up a little lady bug wind-up toy from the counter and handing it to Kara, Ellen led us into the living room. Over by the window, there was a rocker made out of hard rock maple and a bookshelf filled with old hardcover books. On the walls were paintings of the country and lake. Ellen led us into another hallway on the other end and to a door that opened to the back porch.

In the distance there was an idling figure sitting in a wooden lounge chair by a couple of trees holding a cold drink facing an endless landscape of blue water. A squirrel ran across the lawn and Kara's eyes widened.

"You see the squirrel?" asked Ellen. "Kara, did you see the squirrel?"

Ellen looked over at us. "We get rabbits around here all the time too and possums. I have this one possum I feed every weekend."

We passed colorful finger paintings, which were clipped to a clothesline on the porch by clothes pins, and came up from behind Gibbs in feet gliding the tops of the short grass.

"Jim!" shouted Ellen, who stayed behind on the porch with Kara.

The figure quickly rose from the chair and approached in shadows.

"You made it," said Gibbs, harnessing a great big grin. "Welcome to the country."

We each took turns shaking each other's hand excitedly with the promise of a long night ahead. I looked over at Griffin as Gibbs began to ask questions about the trip up from the city.

"Why don't you fix some cold drinks," yelled Ellen. "You can ask questions later."

"What do you guys want?" asked Gibbs, presumably with the intent to please us with a vast array of cold beverages from inside the house.

"I got beer, soda—I just made myself a Manhattan," he said with excitement. "Do you want Manhattans?"

"I'll take one," said Griffin.

"I'll have one too," I said, staring at a duck in the water.

Gibbs turned around to look at what I was staring at.

"Sometimes we get geese too," he said.

"I have lemonade in the kitchen if anyone wants it," yelled Ellen.

"I'm making Manhattans," said Gibbs.

"Manhattans?" asked Ellen. "But it's ten-thirty in the morning."

"It's five o'clock somewhere in the world," said Gibbs, walking toward the porch.

To say that Gibbs and Ellen had a relationship built on constant power struggles disguised as battles in a larger waged war is to be very modest. For instance, I remember one day Gibbs had told me he was going to have Lou Malnati's pizza for dinner for the first time, following a discussion we had about the best pizza places in Chicago.

"We're going to have Lou's tonight," he had said very convincingly. I think he said it more to convince himself. He repeated it several more times to himself just as convincingly.

The next day, when I met Gibbs for lunch I had asked how he liked the pizza.

"Oh, we didn't have it," he had said. "Ellen made spaghetti." I remember he had said it in a defeated way.

We followed Gibbs back to the porch and as he started to make the drinks, I looked out at the lake. It was as peaceful as Gibbs had described. Griffin began to tell Gibbs about the traffic in the city.

"This is rush hour, my friends," said Gibbs, smiling.

"So how's studying going?" asked Ellen, who was now sitting down with Kara at the porch table with a glass of lemonade.

"Fine," I said.

Griffin nodded in agreement.

"I remember when Jim was studying last year for it," she said. "I was planning the wedding and I was eight months pregnant with Kara. I had to do it all myself. I told Jim—study—I don't want you to have to take it in February."

Gibbs handed us the drinks with accentuated passes.

"I'll have one later when Robin and Laura get here," said Ellen to anyone wondering why she wasn't having one.

"All right, boys," said Gibbs, lifting his drink in a toast. "To good times."

"To good times," Griffin and I said together, toasting our glasses.

Ellen lifted her lemonade ceremoniously into the air and took a sip.

"Did Jim tell you about The Cove?" asked Ellen.

"The Cove?" I asked.

"It's a grill and bar on this island across the way," said Gibbs. "We'll take the boat to it later. You float to it and dock up to the post and walk right up to the bar. You guys will like it."

"I've got to play my game at the bar," said Ellen. "They have this game called Quick Draw where you pick a number and a ball on an electronic screen and it bounces and if it hits your number you win money and if you bet on more than one you win more money. It's so much fun."

The day wore on and as the sun spawned the air directly above in a yellow country haze, Ellen's two friends, Robin and Laura, arrived and we all got on the boat and pushed off from the pier. Ellen held Kara, who had suddenly become enthralled with a seagull flying above. Robin and Laura sat in twin casual poses with visors and sun block glistening arms, looking out at the water as if waiting to be entertained by us or the seagulls, and whichever one it was wouldn't, I don't think, have mattered the slightest bit.

"Let's all talk about something," said Ellen.

"Okay," I said.

"What does everyone want to talk about?" she asked. "Look at that cloud," she shouted. "Isn't that one of the most magnificent cloud formations you've ever seen?"

I looked up at the cloud she was pointing to in the sky and it was white and billowy and outlined in gold rims from the sun. We were all staring up at the sky when Gibbs said, "She gets excited about clouds."

"Excited?" said Ellen. "Tom, is it or is it not one of the most magnificent clouds you've ever seen?"

"It's pretty magnificent I have to say," I said, feeling like I had to strongly agree at that moment.

Kara just then cried, having dropped her little lady bug wind-up toy, and there was no more discussion about the cloud.

As the boat drifted across the water, Griffin started to talk about his father's boat.

"He keeps it at Monroe Harbor," he said. "It's a small sailboat. A glorified dinghy. You can fit about six people on it. Seven is pushing it. Six is kind of pushing it."

As the boat approached the dock jetting out from the island, Gibbs tied a sailor's knot at the end of a rope.

"This is where Jim shows everybody how to make a sailor's knot," said Ellen. "If Jim doesn't know anything else, he knows his sailor's knots and his Manhattans and sometimes his knots are better because of his Manhattans."

Gibbs swung the rope around the docking post and jumped out onto the dock, pulling the line on the boat until it was horizontal to the edge. As we stepped from the boat to the dock, Ellen leaned forward and whispered in my ear.

"Do you want to know something about Jim?"

"Sure," I said.

"Jim only likes Manhattans because my father drinks them," she said.

The sun flared through the trees as we walked around the bar to a set of tables on the lawn near the water. We pushed two tables together and sat down, boys on one side and girls on the other like a junior high school dance.

"This is so funny," said Ellen, noticing the seating arrangement. "Isn't this funny? Tom, come sit next to Robin. Griffin, sit next to Laura."

I stood up and sat next to Robin while Griffin brought his chair over to Laura.

"That's better," said Ellen. "Isn't that better?"

We sat quietly, basking in the warm glow of the sun in our newly assigned seats, looking peacefully about. Later, Gibbs held Kara when Ellen went to the bar with Robin and Laura to play the numbers game that she had mentioned earlier while we stayed at the table and talked about the hot dog eating contest held at Coney Island that afternoon.

"Joey Chestnut won again," said Griffin. "That's two years in a row."

Griffin wiped the sweat from the side of his face.

"It might be three," said Griffin.

"Have you ever tried white hots before?" asked Gibbs.

Griffin and I both shook our heads.

"They're hot dogs that I've only seen in upstate New York," said Gibbs. "They're the best."

"We can have hot dogs tonight too if you want them," said Ellen, who had come back from the bar with Robin and Laura. Ellen took Kara from Gibbs and sat down at the table. "I don't think we have any. We'd have to go get some."

It was around three o'clock as we floated across the water back toward the dock in front of the cottage. After several slightly different conversations about dinner, Gibbs and Griffin decided to go to the store to get some hot dogs and buns while I stayed to help Ellen start the grill.

"Ah, air conditioning," said Robin, her face red from the heat, as we stepped inside the kitchen. She took her visor off and tried to give some life to her matted down hair with a moving hand. "I'm glad I waited to shower."

"I have a blister on the side of my foot," said Laura, sitting down and inspecting it. "I wore the wrong shoes."

"I guess the beef sandwiches aren't enough," said Ellen, walking out the back door toward the grill on the porch. "But I guess I kind of made my own bed by opening the door."

She leaned over to ignite the grill and as it turned, there was a clicking noise, but it wouldn't light. She tried several more times and then I tried as well, and though it ignited for a moment, it didn't remain lit.

"I don't think Jim has his phone with him," said Ellen, as if she was thinking out loud. "I'm just going to go to the gas station to exchange the tank."

"I'll go with you," I said.

We walked around to the front of the house. As I carried the propane tank, Ellen held Kara.

There was a neighbor out on the front lawn with a couple of children.

"I thought I heard you," started Ellen. "Are you going to the fireworks later?"

"We sure are," said the neighbor. "You?"

"Yeah," said Ellen. "It should be fun."

Ellen had parked down the street to keep the driveway open for us. She unlocked the doors of the hot car and as I secured the propane tank on the floor in the backseat, she buckled Kara, who was holding her little lady bug wind-up toy, in her child's seat.

I sat down in the passenger seat as Ellen blasted the air conditioning and we started down the bend in the street.

"Both Jim and I are small town at heart," said Ellen. "Jim grew up in Lake Valley, which is 3,000 people and I grew up in a neighboring small town called River Oak. We like the small town feel and coming here on the weekends is nice, even though big money is around and a lot of the people live in the city and come here on the weekends like us."

She wiped her forehead.

"I miss having neighbors just stopping by for a hot dog out of the blue," she said. "I wish the neighbors would just stop by. I had that growing up."

Kara started to cry.

"We're almost there, honey," said Ellen. "Just a couple of more blocks."

"Kara seems like she is very high-energy," I said.

"She is," said Ellen. "She runs everywhere, and doesn't ever want to take a nap. She's a little firecracker."

I looked back over my shoulder at Kara, who had calmed down.

"She loves swimming," said Ellen, who I knew had been a competitive swimmer in college.

Ellen looked in the rearview mirror at Kara.

"Don't you Kara?" asked Ellen.

There was no response.

"I didn't start until I was three," said Ellen. "She's got a two year start on me."

A car turned out onto the street from the gas station as we pulled up to a pump on the far end.

"I need gas for my car at the same time," said Ellen. "Would you mind pumping it as I exchange the tank?"

"Sure," I said.

I lifted the tank out of the car and carried it to the attendant's station and left it on the floor, and then headed back to the pump.

At about four-thirty, Ellen began to set appetizers out on the porch table. As she came around, she urged Gibbs to make everyone a new drink.

Ellen was now wearing a black "Group Therapy" blouse with a picture of three cocktails drawn in glitter and rhinestones.

"You're quite sparkly in the sun," said Laura, looking up at her from the porch table.

"I know," said Ellen, pointing to the kitchen window. "I'm watching myself in my reflection."

I stood next to Gibbs staring at the moss on a nearby rock as he started to make the drinks. As I looked west, the sun clung to a deep sky with red and orange streaks.

"You don't see a sky like that in the city," said Gibbs.

I nodded in agreement.

"I'm waiting for my basil to become more leafy so I can make pesto," said Ellen to Griffin, who was looking at her little garden.

"Growing up, we would have a block party and the entire neighborhood would cook out," Robin said to Laura in an exclusive conversation.

In everyone's hand there was a cold drink in a glass with lots of ice. On the table there was a large Lazy Susan with apple slices, pineapple, blueberries, green grapes, purple grapes and cherries along the edges and yogurt dip in the middle.

When Gibbs asked Ellen if there was a spoon to take the fruit, she pushed a little box of toothpicks toward him.

"Introduce yourself to the toothpicks," she said.

"I'm not going to use a toothpick for every piece of fruit I want," said Gibbs, turning around and walking into the kitchen to get a spoon.

At six-thirty, the last hot dog came off the grill. As everyone sat back in the early evening air to digest, there were merging conversations about the economy and politics and news from that week.

"Tell me, Tom, how bad is the job market now?" asked Ellen. "I tell Jim he should be happy he has a job. I hear about lawyers being laid off every week, not associates, but partners."

"It's a bad time to graduate," I said.

As I reached for a bottle of water, I started to listen to Griffin tell Robin and Laura a story from law school.

"One time we had a partner from a big firm come to our trial advocacy class as a guest judge," he said. "It was a night class and he was going to critique our presentations. We were all giving power point presentations and I was up first and I was setting up the computer and the projector and I remember he put his head flat down on the desk and said, 'God, am I fucking tired.'"

They snickered in a cool sort of way.

"He kept his head flat down on the desk for almost thirty seconds and then sat up just as I got ready to begin and said, 'Let's go,'" said Griffin.

Griffin sipped his drink.

"I remember later questioning whether I'd be able to work eighty hour weeks like him," said Griffin. "At that point, it's just money. Eighty hour weeks. I could probably do that for two years and pay off my loans, but I would think if you did that for a long time you would burn out or you would find yourself sitting in a trial advocacy class at some law school as a guest judge with your head flat down on the desk for nearly thirty seconds saying, 'God am I fucking tired' to a bunch of law students."

As the evening started to hint of darkness, Ellen came out with a small candled cake for Kara and everybody sang happy birthday to her. Gibbs snapped twenty pictures from the same angle and then took one step to his right and snapped twenty more. Ellen cut the first piece for Kara—a corner that had a little butterfly made out of white and yellow frosting, and then she cut generous pieces for the rest of us.

"I'm having a conversation with myself not to eat cake," said Robin.

"How's it going?" asked Laura.

"I'll tell you later," said Robin.

At eight-thirty, we all walked down to the pier carrying lawn chairs and a cooler in little steps through the fresh summer night air. The fireworks were going to be shot from a barge in the middle of the lake and as the sun fell more and more into darkness all the families that had cottages along the lake headed outside and waited for it to begin.

In a sky of vast blackness, the first shell shot up and over the lake and broke into a panorama of color and noiseless glitter, stirring ghosts of revolutions past hushed only by the gentle breeze. As an ensuing series of blasts crushed the black sky with splashes of bright, glamorous color, Kara "ooed" and "ahhed" at the noiseless colorful ones and hid her face under a Frisbee from the thunderous bangs of the loud ones.

After the fireworks, Ellen, Robin and Laura went inside to put Kara to sleep while Gibbs, Griffin and I stayed out on the porch and reminisced about law school. Later, I was watching a firefly light up in flashes of beautiful light across the dark landscape when Gibbs asked whether Griffin and I wanted another Manhattan. As Gibbs stood up, Griffin smacked himself on his leg, crushing a mosquito into his flesh. Its guts spread across his palm in an thin red smear.

Gibbs asked again whether we wanted another Manhattan. It had been a night crowded with Manhattans. We had been drinking them steadily since ten-thirty. In the moonlight, I could see Gibbs leaning forward—his staggering shadow outlined in good graces.

"I'm starting to get eaten alive," said Griffin. "I think I'm done."

Gibbs nodded, the ice in his glass clinking. He then looked over toward me.

"Me too," I said. "I'm beat."

At two in the morning, the night broke with a cry for help. Through the thick blanket of country air, footsteps rushed through the hallway. Light seeped into rooms from bottoms of doors while panicked voices bruised serenity in an eruption of shouts and slammed doors. As I raised my head, I thought perhaps Gibbs was sleepwalking again or something to that effect, but when I opened the door to my bedroom to see what the chaos what about, Gibbs was standing in forced ease holding Kara, who was in a catalytic state. Her eyes were almost at the top of her head and her teeth kept clamping down on Gibbs's finger, which was knuckle-deep in Kara's mouth to prevent her from biting down on her own tongue.

"It's Kara," said Gibbs in a cracked, uncertain voice. "She's had a seizure."

I looked over at Kara in worry.

"The ambulance is on its way," he said, collecting himself. "Can you go to the front window and tell me when it comes because I can't see it from the hallway?"

I nodded and raced over to the window in my bedroom and watched
the street. Griffin's door cracked open from across the hallway. He came over, squinting from the light.

"What's going on?" he whispered.

"Kara had a seizure," I said. "I told Gibbs I would tell him when the ambulance arrived."

He nodded without saying anything.

Lights flashed across the black landscape and a moment later the ambulance pulled up to the house in a cloud of dust.

"It's here!" I yelled. "The ambulance is here!"

There were feet rushing on hardwood floors as the front door flung open, and as we watched from the window, Gibbs ran out to the ambulance with Kara cradled in his arms. One paramedic held the back door of the ambulance open and helped Gibbs inside. Ellen followed right behind them. The other paramedic closed the door after she was inside and then ran around to the front of the ambulance and drove off in hurried dust clouds until it was swallowed by the night.

A long silence soon followed.

"I couldn't do what he's doing," said Griffin, finally, as he continued to stare out the window at the blackness in a state of shock. "I couldn't be a father right now and be responsible for something like that. I mean I still feel like a kid."

"I know what you mean," I said, nodding.

Through the walls of the bedroom we could hear Robin and Laura talking in hurried patterns of speech.

"As you look at tonight, as you think about what just happened, do you ever worry whether you might be, for instance, the next Gibbs?" asked Griffin. "How often do you think about the future?"

"Sometimes it feels like it's all I do lately," I said. "And in all honesty, I'm tired of waiting for it. And I'm beyond tired if studying."

He nodded.

"All I'd like is to get away—forget about the exam and go far, far away," I said. "For a little while."

"Do you want to know something?" he asked.

"Sure," I said.

"I don't know if I want to practice law," he said. "In fact, lately, I've been questioning whether I should even take the bar exam."

"What?" I said astonished.

"I think I'm burnt out," he said. "I don't know what's the matter with me. I did some of the practice questions yesterday and wasn't getting any of them right."

"Which level were you doing?" I asked.

"The hardest one," he said.

"You're not supposed to be getting all of those right," I said.

"Yeah, but usually I can read something once and I remember it," he said. "It's not like I have a photographic memory or anything, but you know? It's just not sticking."

He sighed.

"Anyway, I've fallen way behind in the study schedule," he said.

I looked at him silently.

"Well, you were just saying you were tired of studying, no, you said you were beyond tired of studying and all you wanted to do was go far, far away—"

"I was just talking," I broke in. "I wouldn't think about not taking the exam."

"I hate litigation and transactions are boring," he said, his eyes flashing about. "I don't want to be Gibbs in five years—stuck at a firm because of school loans and a kid."

His voice broke off.

"But I don't want to be Connor either," he said. "I don't know what I want."

"Connor?" I said. "What does he—"

"He's older than me and he still doesn't know what he wants to do with his life," he said. "It's like he's making a last desperate attempt to be someone he's not for this girl. He is obsessed with this girl. He's lost weight and he's buying new clothes and new shoes. He's like a girl! I find the whole thing, if you really want to know, depressing."

He looked out the window at the moon and the light falling in the night.

"You know he told me the other day he wants to get his Masters in Taxation because he wants a degree from a better school on the top of his résumé?" he said. "I could never do that. I could never do something without a purpose. That's why I don't know whether I'm going to take the exam. If I'm not going to practice, what's the use?"

I sat there for a moment digesting what he had said. Suddenly, the moon looked very old as I looked at it in the sky.

"I need to get away," said Griffin. "Far away. For a little while. I need time to think. That's why I'm going to Colombia."

"You're going where?" I asked.

"Cartagena," he said. "To be exact."

"When?" I asked.

"August," he said. "For two weeks."

"Do your parents know?" I asked, knowing they wouldn't continue paying his mortgage if they knew he wasn't going to take the exam and they certainly wouldn't pay for a trip to Colombia.

"Yes, but they think I'm going to take the exam first," he said under an assumed air of indifference.

"What are you going to tell them in October when the results come out?" I asked.

"I'm just going to tell them I failed it," he said. "By then, I'll hopefully know whether I'm going to study for the February exam or, I don't know, do something else."

"Are you going alone?" I asked.

He shook his head.

"Blair?" I asked.

"Yeah," he said with blinking eyes. "She knows somebody who owns a hostel in Panama City where we can stay for free. And then I found a boat that we can take to Colombia."

I stood there in quiet awe looking at the moon and the blackness around it. We talked for another hour and then Griffin shuffled back to his room and I fell asleep watching the stars.

Several days later, Gibbs caught up with me back in Chicago on the phone and told me that Kara was out running around again. He said that the doctors thought that she had had a reaction to the flu shot she was given the afternoon prior to the incident and didn't think she would be prone to epileptic seizures.

Within a week, Griffin stopped going to class completely. He told me that he called the Illinois Bar and officially deferred the exam until February. His plan was now to drift for the rest of July.

That Friday, I went to work and filled out a leave of absence form for the two weeks immediately before the exam. At noon, Jerry was cheerfully on his way to lunch when I ran into him.

"I'll take the elevator with you to the lobby," he said, his arms hanging stiffly down along his sides.

As we waited for the elevator, he asked me how studying was going and we chatted a little about the Cubs and then he started telling me about his weekend.

"I actually had a very productive weekend," he said as a vague happiness swept over his face. "I packed and got ready for my move; I just bought a place in River North and closed on it last Tuesday."

As the elevator arrived, the doors opened and we stepped inside. In a quiet stretch, the elevator swooped down to the lobby, letting everyone out. I was heading toward the door when Jerry said, "Let's buy a lottery ticket."

"All right," I said after a slight hesitation.

"Whenever I buy a lottery ticket," started Jerry, "I think ahead of time, 'What would I do if I won?'"

"What would you do?" I asked, following him into the small convenient store near the south entrance of the building.

"Well, certainly, I'd quit my job," said Jerry, turning to me. "I'd start a jazz band. I like rock, but if I'm going to play, it would be jazz. I went to a concert at Millennium Park recently. It was a jazz band and I sat there and listened. I loved it."

On the following Thursday, I met with Gibbs for lunch at a crowded sandwich shop on Madison and Dearborn, a favorite spot of mine, for a couple of elaborate sandwiches. It was not yet noon and the sandwich shop rang with chatter and laughter and enthusiastic introductions to lunch meetings. Slats of glowing sunshine streaked through the window, creating a bright shaft of light across our table.

"Since the last time I saw you, there's no other way to say it," said Gibbs, pausing. "I had a complete nervous breakdown."

I looked at him without breath.

"I was hospitalized for eight days," he said. "I really thought I was going to be in a psychic ward for the rest of my life. I thought I was nuts. But I'm fine now. They put me on Xanax four times a day. It's a very low dosage."

He glanced impatiently around the restaurant.

"Did I tell you Kara had another seizure?" he asked.

His voice held me silent for a moment longer.

"No," I said. "When?"

"Several days after the fourth," he said as sweat pooled over his brow. "But it's not just that. I was having anxiety attacks. I mean, at one point, I thought I was having a heart attack."

He leaned forward confidentially.

"The doctor said it is very common for someone my age and in my profession, and especially with Kara's situation, to have anxiety attacks," he said. "But I'm fine now. The doctor said the dosage is so low that he will eventually wean me off of it."

"Did the firm know?" I asked.

He nodded.

"I called in sick three times," he said. "They weren't thrilled. I couldn't lie to them. I told them I had to be hospitalized to have my heart checked because I was having panic attacks. They're not going to fire me at this point. I've already passed the point where I'm making money for them rather than costing them money."

As his voice faded off, there was a pause.

"So what about you?" he said quickly changing the subject. "What's new with you?"

"Ah," I stammered, "nothing."

I lowered my head and traded glances with the room.

"Want to go for a walk?" I asked, starting to feel eavesdropping at neighboring tables.

"Ah, no, I'm all right," he said, misreading my face in the confusion.

"Well, it's just because I'm inside all day every day studying," I said, my words running together.

"All right," he agreed.

I stood up and threw my sandwich wrapper away into the trash canister and waited calmly by the door.

"I don't look crazy, do I?" he whispered, quickly following.

There was an awkward beat.

"No," I said reassuringly.

We walked outside into the heat of the noonday sun and shouldered the crowds on the busy street.

"You know, you have to come up to the cottage again sometime this summer," he said, attempting to lighten the mood. "Maybe after the bar exam."

"Sure," I said, nodding.

He wiped the gathering sweat from his brow.

"My father-in-law, by the way, put me in contact with someone at a small firm in Country Lakes," he said. "I told him it was time for me to spread my wings."

He hesitated.

"I don't think I can do this much longer," he said with an impassioned look. "It's killing me. It's actually killing me."

He wiped the sweat from his brow again.

"If I didn't have Kara," he said, pausing.

"Yeah, I think you need to find a healthier environment," I said.

"Ah, Tom, remember a couple of years ago I was up and coming," he said. "I was alive. I had a future. I feel like a beaten man. I need to get back to being that other person somehow."

We wandered around the block for a long time under wisps of a slow breeze and the sound of the passing traffic and then casually shook hands and parted ways, entering our respective tall, stuffy buildings with a view of the city where the people below on the street looked like ants.

The next week went by in long sleepless pitches of time. On the following Tuesday, the harsh yellow glare of the sun beamed across a maturing afternoon sky as I met Gwynn at a small restaurant to study.

"Nobody's gonna judge," said Gwynn in her phone, holding a hand to her forehead. "Nobody would ever judge anybody on that."

She took a long breath.

"Oh, God, that's horrible," she said. "Yeah, I sent a text to her this morning. I called her last night and left a voicemail and I sent a text to her this morning. She probably needs her space."

I sat there quietly looking out the window at the street, listening to her conversation.

"All right, I will talk to you later," she said. "Bye."

Gwynn pressed a button on her phone to end her conversation and turned to me.

"Jaclyn is freaking out about the exam," she said as she ran her hand through her hair. "She really thinks she's going to fail. She like won't answer her phone."

She hesitated.

"The other day Tanya was in a hysterical laughter the entire day," she said. "She kept saying, 'I'm totally going to fail.' My friend Aimee, who you know from class, well, she decided yesterday when she was studying that her humidifier was too noisy and that moment went out to the store and bought a new one."

The server came forward. "Are you two ready?" she asked.

"I'm not going to eat," she said, looking at me sullenly.

"Really?" I asked. "Did you have a late lunch?"

"I had bread around twelve o'clock yesterday afternoon," she said.

"You know what? Can you give us a few minutes?" I asked the server.

"Sure," she said, turning away.

"Are you all right?" I asked Gwynn, studying her eyes.

"Yeah, I think I'm just hitting my wall," she said tightly.

She pushed her hair back with a faraway look in her eyes.

"I'm not going to cry," she said, sounding sulky. "I am not going to cry."

"Let's do something different today," I said after a pause. "I think we can both use a little break from studying tonight."

Honest surprise washed over her face.

"Like what?" she asked, clenching her flashcards in her hands tightly as if they were all the world's gold.

"You can take your flashcards with you if you'd like," I said.

"My mom served store-bought lasagna before to company," said Gwynn, who in the setting sun had never looked so beautiful.

We sat in upright sitting poses on a big red blanket in Grant Park at slow dusk eating fast food lasagna out of plastic containers among summer sounds and the warm air and waited with a growing idling crowd of people on blankets and lawn chairs under the hum of many conversations on the cut grass for the movie *Some Like It Hot* to begin on the enormous white screen that stretched across the northeastern corner of the park.

"It was for some cousins that told her they were coming, giving her a day and a half notice, and she was like, 'I don't have enough time to pull it all together,'" she said with some theatrics. "So, she went to the store and bought one of the large frozen lasagnas and dumped it in one of her large trays and she sprinkled some of her own parmesan cheese and some fresh Italian seasoning on top and made her own salad and fruit salad and nobody ever knew."

"But you knew?" I asked flatly.

"Yeah, my brother and I knew," she said with a more relaxed look on her face.

"You should have complemented her at the table," I said.

"Yeah," she said as a smile touched her lips. "I think my brother did. No, but they were complementing her on the lasagna and my mother was like, 'Oh, thank you. It was nothing.' You should have seen the detail she went into to cover up her tracks. She had me take the kitchen trash with the box from the lasagna into the garage just in case one of them had to throw anything away so they wouldn't see the box from the lasagna sitting there."

At about eight-thirty, the balance between early darkness and a fledgling twilight had been struck and as the movie started, Gwynn reached for my hand. The breeze off the lake had pleasantly cooled the warmed air while high above the bright glint of the crescent-shaped moon shined across an evening sky crowded with sparkling stars. In the middle of the movie, in the moonlight, I caught sight of a single, lanky silhouette that I knew had to be the shadowed outline of Jerry. It was an invisible, lonely soul looking for a friendly nod from the moon. As usual, he was standing near a group of people, but he didn't appear to be with anyone. He stood there all night, laughing at the parts of the movie that were funny while gripping the edge of the railing he was leaning against during the action scenes. The more I watched him, the tighter I held Gwynn's hand in the dark and when the credits flashed onto the screen I looked over, but he had vanished.

July pushed on with many still nights at the coffee shop and with the exam a week away, Connor and I started studying separately in knots of unease. Three days before the exam I saw him at the coffee shop and he looked like he had lost another five pounds.

"You want to grab lunch?" I asked.

"I can't," he said as he attempted to type a random, genius remark on Facebook. "I have someone coming to my apartment to clean at two-thirty for this weekend. A maid."

"How long is she going to be there?" I asked.

"Two hours," he said. "I have a small place. It's a one bedroom. I pay her forty dollars. I go into my bedroom and close the door and when she's finished with the bathroom and the kitchen and the living room, she goes into the bedroom and I go out there."

He quickly checked his phone.

"I don't watch her," he said, slightly distracted. "I feel guilty."

"Are you afraid she might steal something?" I asked.

"I have nothing for her to steal," he said, raising his face.

"How did you find her?" I asked.

"Craigslist," he said. "Listen, so do you want to hear the latest?"

"Sure," I said.

He turned toward me.

"All right, so apparently, Courtney—remember I told you she has this new boyfriend?"

"Right," I said.

"Well, apparently, she's going to bring him to Chicago this weekend," he said.

"Why is she bringing him?" I asked.

"I don't know if she is bringing him or whether he wanted to come to see her off, but he's coming—they're coming—on Saturday," he said.

"And you leave for the trip—," I started.

"Sunday," he broke in. "We leave Sunday."

The muscles around his lips tightened.

"Listen," he said, leaning forward anxiously toward me, planting his elbows on the table and touching the tips of his fingers together. "I've talked to Griffin. This is what I think we're going to do. This Saturday is Venetian Night. Griffin already said we can take his father's boat onto the lake to watch the boat parade and fireworks. What are you doing that night? Now that she's bringing him, I kind of want to have some friends there with me to outnumber him and kind of shift the attention away from me and Courtney. Griffin is already coming with that girl, Blair."

"When is it?" I asked.

"Saturday," he said.

I had a curious wish to see Connor's plan through. Still, I hesitated for a moment.

"Sure," I said, finally.

Over the next couple of days, I lost touch with everyone and tramped back and forth from my apartment to the coffee shop. One night, I was in bed facing the wall and I could hear my father's voice and all the advice he had given to me through the years. The day before the exam, I tried to avoid people in general. I was not in the mood to be drawn into a fake series of greetings with people I slightly knew.

At seven o'clock that night, Adam called with Lilly to wish me luck.

"Um, Uncle Thomas?" asked Lilly.

"Yes, Lilly?" I said.

"Um, I forgot," said Lilly.

I heard Adam whispering to her on the other end of the phone to wish me good luck on the exam.

"Oh, yeah, um, good luck on the exam," said Lilly.

"Thank you, Lilly," I said.

My parents called me as well on speakerphone and sent simultaneous good wishes. Barbara called me later that night and left a message.

About nine o'clock, with vague dread, I remember I went for a walk along Rush Street to clear my head of the immensity of the moment and watched the ghostly moon parade through passing clouds in the night while people with pressing needs shouldered by me on the street in urgent walks. There were noisy cars, and as I turned down a quiet corner, I closed my eyes to a vision of the future and felt the gorgeous breeze gently flap at my face.

On the morning of the exam, jumbled bits of sunshine broke across the silent plane in a slow yellow glaze along the horizon. In the early stillness, I awoke with my head creasing the luxurious ball of my lumped pillow. I showered quickly under passing thoughts of despair, dressed and went to the door and paused there a second while reflecting on the moment in a philosophical way.

The test site was at a hotel downtown, which faced east on Michigan Avenue. I sat in the last row on the right side of the room. The seats on the left side filled slowly as proctors directed students milling about to vacant spots. The bar exam was divided into four three hour sessions over two days; on both days there was a three hour morning session, an hour lunch break, and then a three hour afternoon session. The first day concentrated only on essay questions while the second day focused on multiple choice questions.

There were three proctors in charge of administering the exam in our room. After attendance was taken, they walked around the room passing out the exams under a tightening air. Afterward, one of the proctors, a middle-aged woman with brown hair wearing a shapeless black dress, read two pages of detailed instructions and about fifteen minutes later the exam began. At lunch, I ate a sandwich I had brought and sat outside listening to varied conversations between people whom I hardly knew. During the afternoon session, there were window washers with suction cups on their feet. The sound of 'Ker plunk, Ker plunk, Ker plunk,' resonated throughout the room for several minutes. The proctor who had read the instructions earlier that morning shrugged and then started giving an evil eye type of stare toward them as if that would stop them from being so noisy.

That night, I watched a baseball game in a kind of restless lull on my couch. The next day, luckily, passed uneventfully. Everyone turned in their exams, gathered their belongings, and then was excused from the room.

"I can't believe it," said a student behind me to his friend as we walked out from the room. "School's over. Now there's only death and taxes."

The restaurant Gwynn had made reservations at was crowded and there were loud conversations and laughter floating in and around the tables. I realized I was entering the painting of the "dinner crowd" I had so many times mentally painted with my brush during my long walks of solitude along Rush Street while studying for the exam. We sat outside on the sidewalk at a table alongside a flower bed and ordered goat cheese and flatbread.

"What was the constitutional law question again?" I asked.

"Vagueness," she said, sitting cross-legged at the table with open-toed sandals. "Void for vagueness. They both were void for vagueness."

"That's right," I said.

"For me, it was the first essay question in the afternoon and I started to feel good about it," she said.

The server approached and filled our waters.

"Have you talked to your parents?" I asked.

She nodded as she reached for a piece of the flatbread.

"I called my mom on Tuesday night to tell her about the first day and it went straight to voicemail and I was like, 'No, it's all right to answer if I call you!' I think she was still weary because of last week when I told her not to call anymore when she had called me five times in three days."

She dressed the flatbread in goat cheese.

"This morning I woke up at six and I was like, 'I'm not going to get out of bed.' And so I stayed in bed until noon," she said. "It felt so weird not to have to study, but because I was asked by my friend Dena from back home to be the maid of honor in her wedding last week, I kind of just looked at bridesmaid dresses online all morning not feeling guilty."

She smiled.

"Mitchell liked that I was home all day," she said. "He was like looking at me oddly all day. I pet him all day and finally took him out and squinted at the sun like a vampire. Then I got my nails done," she said showing them off, "oh, and I finished packing."

She stared at her nails a bit longer.

"I can't believe I'm going to be in South Africa in, well, tomorrow at some point," she said. "I can't believe I'm done with law school. I can't believe I don't have to buy anymore books. I guess I have to interview now. That will be fun. It's not like any firm will hire me now without knowing I passed for sure in this market."

The server poured more water into our glasses.

"You know, when I got out of the exam, it was weird," I said. "This guy behind me said to his friend, 'I can't believe it. School's over. Now there's only death and taxes.'"

I hesitated.

"When I went home I started to think about everything and I was like, 'I guess I go to work every day now for the rest of my life,'" I said. "I came to the conclusion right at that moment."

Gwynn smiled.

After dinner, we decided to go for a long walk along the lakefront. In silent stretches, warm air intermingling with faint sweeps of a fresh breeze drew about. We circled Buckingham Fountain, and as we kissed under the sparkle of the stars in almost the same spot as our first kiss, the summer faded into the night where there was a promise of things to come.

The next morning, the vast hot sky painted yellow rims of light through high clouds, casting patterns of shadow on the street. In an attempt to make up some hours that I had missed while studying for the exam, I went to work early. As I entered the office, I saw Jerry from afar passing through the hallway blowing his nose noiselessly.

"So you'll get the results in six weeks?" he asked after an elaborate handshake to welcome me back.

"Yeah," I said. "They said the first week of October. They send an e-mail."

"When we got our bar results back in the day, there was no internet or e-mail," he said. "You'd wait through the summer for an envelope to arrive with the regular snail mail; a fat envelope meant you passed and a thin envelope meant you failed. A thin envelope usually contained a single letter informing one of their failure—'regrettably,' of course. It wasn't that it was any more personal than an e-mail, but you could hold it in your hands before having the guts to actually open it and just study its thickness."

He paused reflectively.

"I remember when mine came; I wasn't home and my mother got it and she held it for me and when I got home later that night I opened it and she had already known that I had passed because she had held it up to the light," he said. "True story."

We talked about his new apartment and whether he felt "settled" and then I asked him whether he had any "big plans" for the weekend.

"I want to rent the first season of *True Blood*," he said, pretending to be cheerful.

"I hear it's good," I said, examining his face, noting the haunting loneliness in his eyes.

"That's what Steven told me too so I think I may get that for tomorrow night," he said, carefully balancing his expressions. "I liked *Dark Shadows* growing up. It's a soap opera about vampires. Have you ever heard of it?"

I shook my head.

"Well, it was before your time," he said, pivoting slightly on his heels. "You know, the original plot of *Dark Shadows* was a governess coming to take care of two possessed children. Have you read *The Turn of the Screw* by Henry James? It's like that. But then the public got infatuated with Barnabas Collins, the reluctant vampire, and the show really became about him."

He hesitated as a rather empty expression washed over his face.

"So, anyway, I think I'll get *True Blood*," he said, lifting his head while pretending to be cheerful again. "Other than that nothing concrete."

It was at that point I asked him whether he wanted to go on the lake with us that Saturday to watch the boat parade on Venetian Night. I think at the time I felt I was inviting him to go with us out of sympathy, but as I now look back on it, I know I did it because, strangely enough, he was my friend.

On that Saturday morning, I went over to Connor's place before going to the Yacht Club. Connor, with two hands shoved in pockets, was pacing back and forth in his living room as if he was walking along an imaginary line. He appeared alternately nervous and hopeful. I could only imagine what he was thinking those last few moments before Courtney arrived. The one great dream he would dream so near it was almost real. I imagined half of him wanted her to march through those doors and declare her unforgotten love for him while the other half wished he was in his room asleep in bed dreaming where the outcome was never in question.

As I watched him turn and pace back and forth in a somewhat fever, I could sense the meditative air of fidelity to his own mission, like the feeling one would have climbing an obscure mountain alone. He had, of course, Courtney's new boyfriend to deal with and he was still fighting with an invisible self from the past.

"You're burning a hole in the floor," I said, finally.

"Am I?" he asked, looking at me with two eyes, but a head that was elsewhere. "I've been doing some thinking," he said. "Should I just tell them to meet us at the dock?"

"They're going to be here any minute," I said.

He looked at me as if I had just taken his toys away from him for not sharing.

"How does the place look?" he asked.

"It looks perfect," I said.

"You don't think it looks too perfect?" he asked, after a slight hesitation. "I mean it doesn't look like I hired a maid to clean my place in order to impress her, right?"

He eagerly awaited my say on the matter as if that would put him out of his current catastrophic thought and allow him to move on to the next one.

"No," I said. "It's—its fine."

"Do you like the shirt?" he asked, pointing to a crisp, new, white button down shirt he wore casually. "I was going to wear yellow, but then I thought, you know, that I should wear white because we were going sailing."

I paused as I studied his shirt, and then nodded. His eyes darted across the room and he went on with his pacing.

"I'm going to call Griffin to make sure he put Jerry's name on the list at the gate," I said.

"Oh, good thinking," he said. "We don't want to be held up in that line tonight."

After a thoughtful pause, he turned and picked up the imaginary line where he had last left it.

I called Griffin while looking down through the window at the spread of the city below.

"Hello?" asked Griffin, answering on the second ring. It sounded like he was already at the Yacht Club as the wind whooshed in sound in the background.

"Hey," I said.

"What's going on?" he asked.

"Did you get my message about Jerry Moss?" I asked as the wind whooshed through the phone again.

I turned around toward the room when I heard Connor break from his imaginary line and I saw him standing before me with his neck slightly tilted back, holding his nose in intense terror. Blood gushed through his fingers and splashed down his arm, smearing across his new crisp white shirt turning it a dark red.

As Griffin started to talk over the outside wind, I broke in— "I'll have to call you back."

"What happened?" I asked Connor incredulously.

He stood with a bewildered and frightened face in a child-like stillness while his hands trembled in absolute mortification.

I ushered him along a new imaginary line—one that led to the bathroom and gave him a handful of tissue. As the blood surged from that thin, tiny vein right on the edge of the left inner faction of his nostril, he held his head back in a miserable tilt as if he was studying the paint on the ceiling. I ran out to grab the yellow shirt he had been considering earlier. When I walked back into the bathroom with it, he was lolling in front of the mirror with the tissue I had given him stuffed into each nostril. It wasn't the least bit amusing. He took the tissue out and started studying it in the mirror.

"I think it stopped," he said, looking closely at it. It had. I handed him some fresh towels from the hall closet and he quickly washed his face and neck. About that time there was a call from the doorman—they were downstairs in the lobby! I handed the phone to Connor and he told the doorman in the most casual voice he could muster given the circumstances, "Let them up." He then finished buttoning his shirt.

As my eyes went over the bathroom it looked remarkably like someone had just hacked another human being to death. I took another towel from the hall closet and wiped up the blood from the bathroom counter and mirror and floor. I even took the red dotted rug that was in there and rolled it up and threw it into a garbage bag along with the bloody towels and then hid it in the back of his bedroom closet.

As I walked back into the living room, Connor, standing in the stiff folds of the bright, yellow button down shirt, began to lean against the wall in an attempt to gather some semblance of composure as he grasped to embrace the reality of the moment. I stood by the window and as I wiped the sweat from my forehead there was a meek knock at the door. Several seconds passed and when I hadn't budged, a thought seemed to have made its way to Connor's head that if he didn't go open the door the meek knocking would continue on forever. A now very dignified Connor strolled effortlessly across the room to the door and when he opened it, I think he almost fainted when he saw that Courtney was alone. I don't actually recall what his initial reaction was when he first saw her, but the next moment he invited her inside with cheerful buoyancy. I met her halfway across the room as Connor attempted to introduce us.

"Is there parking on the street?" she asked.

Connor quietly pulled a smile over a casual tremble in his lips.

"Ian is downstairs with the car," she said. "The doorman was giving him a hard time about leaving it."

I told her I would run down and work it out.

Courtney nodded and then turned to Connor.

"Just so you know Ian hates you. I told him about us in college and he doesn't like that we're going on this trip together."

I took the garage parking pass from the counter and opened the front door. Shutting it behind me, I loped down the hallway toward the elevators. When the doors of the elevator opened in the lobby, there was a tall man talking to the doorman and I asked him if he was Ian.

"Yeah, are you Connor?" he asked with rather superior eyes.

"No, I'm Tom, Tom Sanders—Connor's friend," I said.

"Ian Dyer," he said, reaching his hand out to shake, his eyes softening slightly.

I handed the parking pass to Ian and told him I would go with him to the garage to park the car. Outside a silver shiny foreign car stood on the curb. We buckled ourselves in for the short ride and I directed him around the corner to the garage entrance. We took the ramp down beneath the foundation of the building and handed the attendant the pass. He wrote out a ticket and handed Dyer the stub and we proceeded in a brisk walk toward the elevators.

While we waited, we chatted about their drive to the city. As I studied his face, I sensed an inner intensity veiled by forced facial expressions. The elevator soon arrived, scooping us up and taking us twenty stories to Connor's floor. We could hear the two of them talking in mumbles from the hallway as we advanced to the door. I knocked and there was silence as footsteps approached. When Connor opened the door I noticed his face was slightly red as if he had just been laughing.

Sprits of light shined into the hallway in a broad glare as Connor, who was extremely calm now, stood casually shadowed in front of the door while Courtney, who had her back to us, was precariously bent over and leaning across the couch by the window, looking down at the city from the same view I had been looking at earlier.

"We were just looking out the window," said Connor, as he noticed what it might have looked like from our view.

Connor and Dyer looked at each other for a moment in silence. Just then Connor realized we were all still standing in the doorway.

"What's wrong with me?" said Connor. "Come in. Come in. Ian, right?"

He asked though he very well knew his name.

"I'm glad you could come," said Connor. "I'm glad you could come see us off."

The two men shook hands stiffly as if each were assessing the other's physical strengths while subtracting weaknesses.

"Ian, come quick, check out this view," said Courtney.

Dyer walked obediently to the window, blazing a new imaginary line among the many tangled ones that would be beholden to that evening.

As Connor walked uneasily into the kitchen, his eyes never left the two of them. After a moment or two, I could see Dyer's presence was having an acute affect on him.

"I've never seen anything so beautiful," she said. "I haven't been to Chicago in awhile."

"It's the southeast view," said Connor in a perfect voice, a reminder that it was the better view. "You can almost see the harbor."

Connor walked up behind them. As the three of them stared in fascination out the window at the untold mysteries of the buildings and the gorgeous people out on the street they looked upon, I was beginning to believe none of them had ever looked out a window in a metropolitan city before.

Connor started to say something to Courtney, but then stopped. There was silence for a moment. It was as if now that they were finally together they didn't know how to talk to each other, especially in a room with others where things could be heard rather than flashed privately on small screens. They stood there slightly awkward looking out the window in the silence with their phones in their pockets and heads full of things to say.

As an airplane broke through the sky and floated among the clouds in an endless drift, a light posturing between the two men ensued and they began casually talking about their toys—how big their apartment was, how shiny their car looked, who had a southeast view from their window to a real world unknown—and it all had the feeling like two snobbish salesmen competing to sell a fantastic future Courtney one day could buy. Before they could discuss what they would purchase next with the thousands or millions they would inevitably make one day in the courtroom or, for that matter, whose father could beat up who, I suggested we go downstairs and hail a taxi to the harbor before it got late.

As the taxi pulled up to the Yacht Club, the fresh air off the lake collided with the broiling afternoon. The shore was filled with a sweltering crowd of eyes watching the vastness of the lake as thousands, red from the sun, began staking spots along the edges of Monroe Harbor to ensure views of the boat parade. There were people in lawn chairs, people standing, people sitting on blankets eating sandwiches from picnic baskets and drinking wine from tiny plastic cups. With smells of hamburgers and hot dogs drifting in the early twilight air, kids were running around with glow sticks wrapped around necks like necklaces and wrists like bracelets.

Outside the Yacht Club, a man in a black collared shirt and khaki pants stood at the gate with a clipboard letting people on the dock. As we moved among the many idling figures toward the gate under a rushing sound from Lakeshore Drive, Connor pulled me aside and whispered, "No question he's a default boyfriend for her."

There were boating parties lining the dock along the labyrinth of piers. I watched the flags attached to masts flap in the breeze in a crescendo of sounds. Up on the driveway, cars pulled to the walk and unloaded boxes of food and supplies for dinners and parties onto wheel barrels, which were then pushed to the dock's edge to waiting tenders. Around the bend, there was an outdoor deck facing the lake with round white paper Japanese-style lanterns strewn from a canvas roof and pathways lined with beds of summer flowers; peonies, meadow sage and wild indigo hybrids.

As we walked inside the Yacht Club, a sign just past the door said: 130 Years of Yachting Excellence. On either side of the walls in the hallway glass cases filled with trophies from different races sporting names and years acted as living monuments of one's greatness. In a formal dining room, men in sports coats and women in summer dresses bunched around white clothed tables and ate decadently while on the other side of the club the bar and grill cooked hot dogs and cheeseburgers and club sandwiches in a more casual atmosphere.

Jerry met us in the hallway, his cheeks and forehead slightly red from the sun. He started to tell me about a past fishing trip while we stood and waited for Griffin. People passed in all directions and several minutes later Griffin called and told us to meet him outside on the north side of the dock. In a glare from the hot sun, Griffin, with a cowboy hat crowning his head, came forward and greeted everyone cheerfully while holding a huge bag of ice in his arms. Blair was standing next to him with sunglasses on in pleasant excitement; she moved forward, holding a stack of paper plates and cups in her hands. With reflections of the sun setting on the water, we boarded the boat and shortly thereafter had dinner. The length of the boat was filled; I sat in the back with Griffin and Jerry, Courtney and Connor were directly in front of us and Dyer and Blair sat near the front.

The sun sank, and the color from the sky vanished, blurring the horizon. Dyer finished a beer and took another one as a seagull flew above in a cry. Jerry started to tell me about his past fishing trip again and as I looked down into the depths of the vivid blue water at the gleaming fish, in the haze of the heat, I caught Dyer's cool eyes as they fell on Connor. I started to get the feeling something bad was going to happen and I have thought back about this very moment hundreds of times since and what I know now, of course, is that I was too unsuspecting of the tension and the light philosophizing and the quick glances that were shot between Dyer and Connor in this context. Still, I never would have believed what was coming.

The night gathered in semi-darkness, and as the first stars sparkled in the sky, the boat pushed off casually from the dock. Thirty boats with decorous lights in varied themes paraded the water along Monroe Harbor, and when the last boat passed, fireworks clapped explosions as the sky erupted in slats of bright glittering light.

The night went on, and as a crescent moon shined down, passing boats with inky outlines and roaring music floated in the water like one big party with different rooms drifting off into the night. Griffin steered us around the open water and with the boat pointed to a distant blackness, we drifted under still stars to an unknown address somewhere on the lake where death awaited us.

In the distance, the great circle of light of the Ferris wheel at Navy Pier flashed radiant beams across the lake. I happened to turn my head to watch a large cruise ship cut across the smooth water in front of us, and, thus, I never saw how the struggle on the boat started. By the time I looked over, Dyer already held Connor in a violent chokehold and in a great confusion of fitful movements the two nearly went over sideways.

As the large passing cruise ship forced long foaming waves across the lake, the boat heaved forward. Jerry and Courtney rushed forward together yelling in voices that drowned each other out and there were five on one side of the boat and it began to slant to one side in a terrifying way.

A cry sprang to Griffin's lips.

"The boat!"

Jerry looked up at Griffin as if it was difficult to hear anything over the noisy cruise ship and the pitching water.

"Stay on your side!" Griffin shouted as water swept over.

The stern of the boat rose up wildly and then dropped down in the rush of water. Jerry tried desperately to pry Dyer's arms from Connor's neck, but he wouldn't let go. I sat still—faintly aware of what would happen next. As Griffin struggled to pull Courtney and Jerry to the other side, the boat slanted in a full tilt. I quickly leaned over the other edge in an attempt to make my body heavier, and as I held the side, all of a sudden, the boat heaved and I felt the ground swept from under me as it flipped over in a barbarous and shocking splash!

A flying cooler rushed wildly through the air and bashed the side of my head and I was thrown headlong into the water, driven down into the depth of freezing blackness. I quickly pushed myself up to the surface with a mouth half-full with water. Once my head broke through the plane of the waterline in a violent burst, a rush of air streamed to my nose. I didn't know how long I had been in the water, but I saw the arc lights from a boat about fifty feet away. Gasping for air, I swam toward it. Griffin was already on board. So was Connor and Courtney and Blair and Dyer. A powerful hand reached for my arm and pulled me from the water, dripping, onto the deck. On my hands and knees, I bent over coughing water from my lungs.

"Are you all right?" I heard a voice asking me. "Are you all right?"

I looked over, light-headed and with my teeth chattering, and saw it was the man that had pulled me onto the boat and I nodded.

"That's a pretty nasty cut you got on the side of your head," the man said, holding a white towel that turned a dark shade of red when he pressed it against my forehead.

"Natalie!" yelled the man. "Natalie! Will you hold this? He's bleeding. His head is bleeding."

A forthcoming female presence began to hold the towel against my head in a nurturing manner as my whole body started to shiver from the wind.

"Don't worry," said the man. "The coast guard is on the way. We will get you patched up as soon as we can."

I looked around and saw everyone huddled on the deck except Jerry. There was a searchlight on the water spanning the lake around and when the coast guard boat arrived, divers were sent into the water. They looked for Jerry for hours, but he never came up. It wasn't until the next morning when his body was recovered from the water that the mystery had come to an end.

Rumors ran rampant in the media as accounts of a fight on board the boat circulated in a broad hysteria. There were reports that one man had seen another trying to kiss his girlfriend, while other media outlets reported a dozen or so equally untrue stories. And though I knew the trip to Spain and the thought of Connor and Courtney's past incited Dyer to the violent behavior that had ensued, I guess any one of those circulating media stories could have rung true because, in the end, it was merely a pre-text; at some point that night on the boat Dyer realized that because of Connor's history with Courtney, he was always going to have "the better view" when it came to her, and, so, he had to do something. Later, he claimed he had "too much to drink" and "wasn't thinking clearly."

An investigation ensued and a couple of days later it was officially ruled to be an accident. It had been determined that the boat had been capsized by the force of the larger cruise ship passing by at a high rate of speed. And that was that.

It rained the morning of the funeral, fittingly, perhaps, because it hadn't rained in weeks, but maybe, I thought, the world was that much sadder with one less dream. On the wet streets, bent heads hidden under buckling umbrellas flashed blinking eyes as the wind whipped through the city. I took a cab to the cemetery, and as the driver pulled up to the gates out front, I paid him and then sloshed through puddles to the gravesite.

There was a little canopy in the distance where I could see the rabbi facing a couple rows of chairs. There were a few lawyers I only knew by sight and a handful of others looking at me with eyes without tears. In the front row, just out of reach of the rabbi, was an elderly woman I presumed was Jerry's mother. She sat there looking at the coffin in a lull listening to the rain hit the bare earth. I sat down toward the back, bowing slightly to the others in acknowledgment and listened to a mix of sad voices. I was the only one from the boat that attended the funeral. There were only six of us there altogether.

The service began and the rabbi spoke eloquently about community and the aspirations of man and, finally, the aspirations of this one man. Somehow the great importance I had placed on the bar exam now seemed, on the whole, more trivial than anything. After the service, everyone kind of gathered under a couple of umbrellas and without many parting words walked to the parking lot. It wasn't pity I was feeling, it was part guilt because I had been the one that invited Jerry to come with us on the boat that night and part, well, everything else.

The shiva was at Jerry's mother's apartment in River North on Ontario and Dearborn. I took a taxi over there and walked up the stairs with a small group, my hand on the railing and my eyes on my shoes following the raindrops left from the wet feet that had walked the steps before me.

There was a nice woman at the door who greeted people as they came in and a little boy who took raincoats and hung them up in the front hall closet. I looked around the apartment and saw several of the faces that were at the funeral service. Light jazz music played faintly in the background. It was apparently one of Jerry's favorite albums.

On the dining room table I noticed there was a spread of lox and cream cheese and bagels and on the table up against the window there was a large sweets basket from State Street Bakery. As I stood there, I started to think about the sweets basket Jerry had won from his spinning class that he kept promising to bring to work and the small irony there would be one at his funeral.

Jerry's mother was sitting in a chair looking distraught as a middle-aged woman sat next to her trying to comfort her. I came forward and introduced myself solemnly.

"Tom Sanders?" she said, repeating my name. "I know you. You worked with Jerry."

At that moment, I realized that it was the exact reversal from when I first met Jerry. I imagined Jerry, who didn't have many people he could call as a friend, told his mother all about me. We chatted for several minutes and then I handed her a card that I had brought. She was so taken aback that I had brought a card she opened it right there in front of me.

"A tree?" she said, as tears started to bead at the edge of her eyes.

I had arranged to have a tree planted in Jerry's honor.

As she dabbed around her eyes with a tissue, I saw a glint of hopefulness as if one day she knew she was going to visit that tree.

A couple more people arrived and gave their condolences, but there were perhaps only nine people there all in all. I walked over to the sweets basket and reached for a brownie and got into a conversation with the man standing beside me. He was eating one of the cookies, but he said the brownies were better. We started to talk about our backgrounds and I told him I just took the bar exam and that I was looking for a job. He told me that he was an attorney at a medium-sized firm and that they might be looking to hire a recent graduate in the coming months as the bar exam results came out. We talked for a half-hour more and he gave me his card and told me to call him the following week.

That Monday, I met Gibbs for lunch. I got there before he did and sat down at a table by the window. He arrived full of excitement a few moments later and quickly broke the news that was already spilling across his face.

"I did it!" he exclaimed cheerfully.

"You did what?" I asked.

"I quit," he said, as a glimmer of hope sprung to his eyes.

He went on to tell me with a fierce energy that they had decided to move to Country Lakes. He said he got a job at the small firm there. There was going to be fewer billable hours and a slower life, he said.

"And in two years," he started, "I'm going to highly consider running for that D.A. position."

It was like the old Gibbs I knew from law school—gone was the paper pushing broken down man Gibbs had become and in its place a re-born spirit with a limitless future.

"Here's your extra pickle, sir," said the young-looking server as she placed a small plate with a giant half dill pickle on the table in front of Gibbs.

"Sir?" he said to me, confused, as she walked away.

The expression on his face told me that he suddenly was starting to feel very old.

"Well, I'm apparently a sir, too," I said. "I guess we are the coming generation of sirs."

"I've called my father sir since I can remember," he said, somewhat amused.

He looked across the restaurant still in thought.

After lunch, I walked through the streets downtown. I felt the warmth of the sun on my face and watched the people around me.

So Gibbs was moving, I thought. *He was actually doing it.*

As the sun shined down brightly from the seemingly endless blue sky, I wandered down to the lakefront. With the cars rushing in sound above, I walked under Lakeshore Drive to the beach. As I watched the water sparkle in the mid-afternoon sun, it looked like it held a thousand secrets.

"So many secrets," I murmured.

As I shaded my eyes from the broad glare grazing the water, I started to think about the rooftop party at Griffin's and the promise of the summer that once was. It felt like a lifetime ago. Now the summer was over. Jerry was dead. Connor was chasing a forever, which was a forever away, and Griffin was just chasing. Gwynn was the only thing I felt was right with the universe at that moment and she was half-way around the world in South Africa on a safari.

I took the business card the attorney at the shiva had handed me out from my wallet and stared at the thick, black letters imprinted on its side.

Sometimes, I guess it is just luck, I thought to myself.

I started to think again about Gwynn and then I thought about life. I looked up at the sky, as if for guidance, and I followed a cloud slowly passing overhead with my eyes and I wondered: Was I chasing a forever, which was a forever away, like Connor, or,

was I just chasing, like Griffin? Or was I more like Gibbs—
chasing what was right all along, but always passively and from a
distance like it was only a dream?

A dream is only a dream if you are not awake, I thought to
myself.

Out on the lake, the sun began to splash light in long brush
strokes of color along the horizon as big, white clouds passed
silently in traffic overhead. I started to think about the next day and
the next. The trains would come to the city in the morning and the
buses would drive through the streets...feet would march to work
following the feet in front of them...hands would clutch steaming
coffee cups...the sun would shine a golden tint over the air...long
morning shadows would shorten to stubs by the afternoon...and as
the monolithic buildings that brace the earth in an etched skyline of
seismic wonder stretched farther into the sky of infinite
possibilities, the sky would reach gorgeously to it and the silent
promises of yesterday would awaken to a future tomorrow.